Eleven Minutes

PAULO
COELHO

ELEVEN MINUTES

Translated from the Portuguese
by Margaret Jull Costa

HarperCollins *Publishers* India
a joint venture with

New Delhi

HarperCollins *Publishers* India
a joint venture with
The India Today Group
by arrangement with
HarperCollins *Publishers* Limited

First published in English by HarperCollins *Publishers* 2003

First published in India by HarperCollins *Publishers* India 2003
Third impression 2004

HarperCollins *Publishers*
1A Hamilton House, Connaught Place, New Delhi 110 001, India
77-85 Fulham Palace Road, London W6 8JB, United Kingdom
Hazelton Lanes, 55 Avenue Road, Suite 2900, Toronto, Ontario M5R 3L2
and 1995 Markham Road, Scarborough, Ontario M1B 5M8, Canada
25 Ryde Road, Pymble, Sydney, NSW 2073, Australia
31 View Road, Glenfield, Auckland 10, New Zealand
10 East 53rd Street, New York NY 10022, USA

Printed and bound at
Thomson Press (India) Ltd.

O, Mary, conceived without sin,
pray for us who turn to you. Amen.

Dedication

On 29th May 2002, just hours before I put the finishing touches to this book, I visited the Grotto in Lourdes, in France, to fill a few bottles with miraculous water from the spring. Inside the Basilica, a gentleman in his seventies said to me: 'You know, you look just like Paulo Coelho.' I said that I was Paulo Coelho. The man embraced me and introduced me to his wife and grand-daughter. He spoke of the importance of my books in his life, concluding: 'They make me dream.' I have often heard these words before, and they always please me greatly. At that moment, however, I felt really frightened, because I knew that my new novel, *Eleven Minutes*, dealt with a subject that was harsh, difficult, shocking. I went over to the spring, filled my bottles, then came back and asked him where he lived (in northern France, near Belgium) and noted down his name.

This book is dedicated to you, Maurice Gravelines. I have a duty to you, your wife and grand-daughter and to myself to talk about the things that concern me and not only about what everyone would like to hear. Some books make us dream, others bring us face to face with reality, but what matters most to the author is the honesty with which a book is written.

And, behold, a woman which was in the city, a sinner; and when she knew that Jesus was sitting at meat in the Pharisee's house, she brought an alabaster cruse of ointment.

And standing behind at his feet, weeping, she began to wet his feet with her tears, and wiped them with the hair of her head, and kissed his feet, and anointed them with the ointment.

Now when the Pharisee which had bidden him saw it, he spake within himself, saying, This man, if he were a prophet, would have perceived who and what manner of woman this is which toucheth him, that she is a sinner.

And Jesus answering said unto him, Simon, I have somewhat to say unto thee. And he saith, Master, say on.

A certain lender had two debtors: the one owed five hundred pence, and the other fifty.

And when they had not wherewith to pay, he forgave them both. Which of them therefore will love him most?

Simon answered and said, He, I suppose, to whom he forgave the most. And he said unto him, Thou hast rightly judged.

And turning to the woman, he said unto Simon, Seest thou this woman? I entered into thine house, thou gavest me no water for my feet; but she hath washed my feet with her tears, and wiped them her hair.

Thou gavest me no kiss: but she, since the time I came in, hath not ceased to kiss my feet.

My head with oil thou didst not anoint: but this she hath anointed my feet with ointment.

Wherefore I say unto thee, Her sins, which are many, are forgiven; for she loved much: but to whom little is forgiven, the same loveth little.

Luke 7: 37–47

For I am the first and the last
I am the venerated and the despised
I am the prostitute and the saint
I am the wife and the virgin
I am the mother and the daughter
I am the arms of my mother
I am barren and my children are many
I am the married woman and the spinster
I am the woman who gives birth and she
who never procreated
I am the consolation for the pain of birth
I am the wife and the husband
And it was my man who created me
I am the mother of my father
I am the sister of my husband
And he is my rejected son
Always respect me
For I am the shameful and the magnificent one

Hymn to Isis, third or fourth century BC,
discovered in Nag Hammadi

Once upon a time, there was a prostitute called Maria. Wait a minute. 'Once upon a time' is how all the best children's stories begin and 'prostitute' is a word for adults. How can I start a book with this apparent contradiction? But since, at every moment of our lives, we all have one foot in a fairy tale and the other in the abyss, let's keep that beginning.

Once upon a time, there was a prostitute called Maria.

Like all prostitutes, she was born both innocent and a virgin, and, as an adolescent, she dreamed of meeting the man of her life (rich, handsome, intelligent), of getting married (in a wedding dress), having two children (who would grow up to be famous) and living in a lovely house (with a sea view). Her father was a travelling salesman, her mother a seamstress, and her hometown, in the interior of Brazil, had only one cinema, one nightclub and one bank, which was why Maria was always hoping that one day, without warning, her Prince Charming would arrive, sweep her off her feet and take her away with him so that they could conquer the world together.

While she was waiting for her Prince Charming to appear, all she could do was dream. She fell in love for the first time when she was eleven, en route from her house to school. On the first day of term, she discovered that she was not alone on her way to school: making the same journey was a boy who lived in her neighbourhood and who shared the same timetable. They never exchanged a single word, but gradually Maria became aware that, for her, the best part of the day were those moments spent going to school: moments of dust, thirst and weariness, with the sun beating down, the boy walking fast, and with her trying her hardest to keep up.

This scene was repeated month after month; Maria, who hated studying and whose only other distraction in life was television, began to wish that the days would pass quickly; she waited eagerly for each journey to school and, unlike other girls her age, she found the weekends deadly dull. Given that the hours pass more slowly for a child than for an adult, she suffered greatly and found the days far too long simply because they allowed her only ten minutes to be with the love of her life and thousands of hours to spend thinking about him, imagining how good it would be if they could talk.

Then it happened.

One morning, on the way to school, the boy came up to her and asked if he could borrow a pencil. Maria didn't reply; in fact, she seemed rather irritated by this unexpected approach and even quickened her step. She had felt petrified when she saw him coming towards her, terrified that he might realise how much she loved him, how eagerly she had waited for him, how she had dreamed of taking his hand, of walking straight past the school gates with him and continuing along the road to the end, where – people said – there was a big city, film stars and television stars, cars, lots of cinemas, and an endless number of fun things to do.

For the rest of the day, she couldn't concentrate on her lessons, tormented by her own absurd behaviour, but, at the same time, relieved, because she knew that the boy had noticed her too, and that the pencil had just been an excuse to start a conversation, because when he came over to her, she had noticed that he already had a pen in his pocket. She waited for the next time, and during that night – and the nights that followed – she went over and over what she would say to him, until she found the right way to begin a story that would never end.

But there was no next time, for although they continued to walk to school together, with Maria sometimes a few steps ahead, clutching a pencil in her right hand, and at other times, walking slightly behind him so that she could gaze at him tenderly, he never said another word to her, and she had to content herself with loving and suffering in silence until the end of the school year.

During the interminable school holidays that followed, she woke up one morning to find that she had blood on her legs and was convinced she was going to die. She decided to leave a letter for the boy, telling him that he had been the great love of her life, and then she would go off into the bush and doubtless be killed by one of the two monsters that terrorised the country people round about: the werewolf and the *mula-sem-cabeça* (said to be a priest's mistress transformed into a mule and doomed to wander the night). That way, her parents wouldn't suffer too much over her death, for, although constantly beset by tragedies, the poor are always hopeful, and her parents would persuade themselves that she had been kidnapped by a wealthy, childless family, but would return one day, rich and famous, while the current (and eternal) love of her life would never forget her, torturing himself each day for not having spoken to her again.

She never did write that letter because her mother came into the room, saw the bloodstained sheets, smiled and said:

'Now you're a young woman.'

Maria wondered what the connection was between the blood on her legs and her becoming a young woman, but her mother wasn't able to give her a satisfactory explanation: she just said that it was normal, and that, from now on, for four or five days a month, she would have to wear something like a doll's pillow between her legs. Maria asked if men used some kind of tube to stop the blood going all over their trousers, and was told that this was something that only happened to women.

Maria complained to God, but, in the end, she got used to menstruating. She could not, however, get used to the boy's absence, and kept blaming herself for her own stupidity in running away from the very thing she most wanted. The day before the new term began, she went to the only church in town and vowed to the image of St Anthony that she would take the initiative and speak to the boy.

The following day, she put on her smartest dress, one that her mother had made specially for the occasion, and set off to school, thanking God that the holidays had finally ended. But the boy did not appear. And so another agonising week passed, until she found out, through some schoolfriends, that he had left town.

'He's gone somewhere far away,' someone said.

At that moment, Maria learned that certain things are lost forever. She learned too that there was a place called 'somewhere far away', that the world was vast and her own town very small, and that, in the end, the most interesting people always leave. She too would like to leave, but she was still very young. Nevertheless, looking at the dusty streets of the town where she lived, she decided that one day she would follow in the boy's footsteps. On the nine Fridays that followed, she took communion, as was the custom in her religion, and asked the Virgin Mary to take her away from there.

She grieved for a while too and tried vainly to find out where the boy had gone, but no one knew where his parents had moved to. It began to seem to Maria that the world was too large, that love was something very dangerous and that the Virgin was a saint who inhabited a distant heaven and didn't listen to the prayers of children.

Three years passed; she learned geography and mathematics, she began following the soaps on TV; at school, she read her first erotic magazine; and she began writing a diary describing her humdrum life and her desire to experience first-hand the things they told her about in class – the ocean, snow, men in turbans, elegant women covered in jewels. But since no one can live on impossible dreams – especially when their mother is a seamstress and their father is hardly ever at home – she soon realised that she needed to take more notice of what was going on around her. She studied in order to get on in life, at the same time looking for someone with whom she could share her dreams of adventure. When she had just turned fifteen, she fell in love with a boy she had met in a Holy Week procession.

She did not repeat her childhood mistake: they talked, became friends and started going to the cinema and to parties together. She also noticed that, as had happened with the first boy, she associated love more with the person's absence than with their presence: she would miss her boyfriend intensely, would spend hours imagining what they would talk about when next they met, and remembering every second they had spent together, trying to work out what she had done right and what she had done wrong. She liked to think of herself as an experienced young woman, who had already allowed one grand passion to slip from her grasp and who knew the pain that this caused, and now she was determined to fight with all her might for this man and for marriage, determined that he *was* the man for marriage, children and the house by the sea. She went to talk to her mother, who said imploringly:

'But you're still very young, my dear.'

'You got married to my father when you were sixteen.'

Her mother preferred not to explain that this had been because of an unexpected pregnancy, and so she used the 'things were different then' argument and brought the matter to a close.

The following day, Maria and her boyfriend went for a walk in the countryside. They talked a little, and Maria asked if he wanted to travel, but, instead of answering the question, he took her in his arms and kissed her.

Her first kiss! How she had dreamed of that moment! And the landscape was special too – the herons flying, the sunset, the wild beauty of that semi-arid region, the sound of distant music. Maria pretended to draw back, but then she embraced him and repeated what she had seen so often on the cinema, in magazines and on TV: she rubbed her lips against his with some violence, moving her head from side to side, half-rhythmic, half-frenzied. Now and then, she felt the boy's tongue touch her teeth and thought it felt delicious.

Then suddenly he stopped kissing her and asked:

'Don't you want to?'

What was she supposed to say? Did she want to? Of course she did! But a woman shouldn't expose herself in that way, especially not to her future husband, otherwise he would spend the rest of his life suspecting that she might say 'yes' that easily to anything. She decided not to answer.

He kissed her again, this time with rather less enthusiasm. Again he stopped, red-faced, and Maria knew that something was very wrong, but she was afraid to ask what it was. She took his hand, and they walked back to the town together, talking about other things, as if nothing had happened.

That night – using the occasional difficult word because she was sure that, one day, everything she had written would be read by someone else, and because she was convinced that something very important had happened – she wrote in her diary:

When we meet someone and fall in·love, we have a sense that the whole universe is on our side. I saw this happen today as the sun went down. And yet if something goes wrong, there is nothing left! No herons, no distant music, not even the taste of his lips. How is it possible for the beauty that was there only minutes before to vanish so quickly?

Life moves very fast. It rushes us from heaven to hell in a matter of seconds.

The following day, she talked to her girlfriends. They had all seen her going out for a walk with her future 'betrothed'. After all, it is not enough just to have a great love in your life, you must make sure that everyone knows what a desirable person you are. They were dying to know what had happened, and Maria, very full of herself, said that the best bit was when his tongue touched her teeth. One of the other girls laughed.

'Didn't you open your mouth?'

Suddenly everything became clear – his question, his disappointment.

'What for?'

'To let him put his tongue inside.'

'What difference does it make?'

'It's not something you can explain. That's just how people kiss.'

There was much giggling, pretend pity and gleeful feelings of revenge amongst these girls who had never had a boy in love with them. Maria pretended not to care and she laughed too, although her soul was weeping. She secretly cursed the films she had seen in the cinema, from which she had learned to close her eyes, place her hand on the man's head and move her head slightly to right and left, but which had failed to show the essential, most important thing. She made up the perfect excuse (I didn't want to give myself at once, because I wasn't sure, but now I realise that you are the love of my life) and waited for the next opportunity.

She didn't see him until three days later, at a party in a local club, and he was holding the hand of a friend of hers, the one who had asked her about the kiss. She again pretended that she didn't care, and survived until the end of the evening talking with her girlfriends about film stars and about other local boys, and pretending not to notice her friends' occasional pitying looks. When she arrived home, though, she allowed her universe to crumble; she cried all night, suffered for the next eight months and concluded that love clearly wasn't made for her and that she wasn't made for love. She considered becoming a nun and devoting the rest of her life to a kind of love that didn't hurt and didn't leave painful scars on the heart – love for Jesus. At school, they learned about missionaries who went to Africa, and she decided that there lay an escape from her dull existence. She planned to enter a convent, she learned first aid (according to some teachers, a lot of people were dying in Africa), worked harder in her religious knowledge classes, and began to imagine herself as a modern-day saint, saving lives and visiting jungles inhabited by lions and tigers.

However, her fifteenth year brought with it not only the discovery that you were supposed to kiss with your mouth open, and that love is, above all, a cause of suffering. She discovered a third thing: masturbation. It happened almost by chance, as she was touching her genitals while waiting for her mother to come home. She used to do this when she was a child and she liked the feeling, until, one day, her father saw her and slapped her hard, without explaining why. She never forgot being hit like that, and she learned that she shouldn't touch herself in front of other people; since she couldn't do it in the middle of the street and she didn't have a room of her own at home, she forgot all about the pleasurable sensation.

Until that afternoon, almost six months after the kiss. Her mother was late coming home, and she had nothing to do; her father had just gone out with a friend, and since there was nothing interesting on the TV, she began examining her own body, in the hope that she might find some unwanted hair which could immediately be tweezered out. To her surprise, she noticed a small gland above her vagina; she began touching it and found that she couldn't stop; the feelings provoked were so strong and so pleasurable, and her whole body – particularly the part she was touching – became tense. After a while, she began to enter a kind of paradise, the feelings grew in intensity, until she noticed that she could no longer see or hear clearly, everything appeared to be tinged with yellow, and then she moaned with pleasure and had her first orgasm.

Orgasm!

It was like floating up to heaven and then parachuting slowly down to earth again. Her body was drenched in sweat, but she felt complete, fulfilled and full of energy. So that was what sex was! How wonderful! Not like in erotic magazines in which everyone talked about pleasure, but seemed to be grimacing in pain. And no need for a man, who liked a woman's body, but had no time for her feelings. She could do it on her own! She did it again, this time imagining that a famous movie star was touching her, and once more she floated up to paradise and parachuted down again, feeling even more energised. Just as she was about to do it for a third time, her mother came home.

Maria talked to her girlfriends about her new discovery, not saying that she had only discovered it a few hours before. All of them – apart from two – knew what she was talking about, but none of them had ever dared to raise the subject. It was Maria's turn to feel like a revolutionary, to be the leader of the group, inventing an absurd 'secret confessions' game, which involved asking everyone their favourite method of masturbation. She learned various different techniques, like lying under the covers in the height of summer (because, one of her friends assured her, sweating helped), using a goose feather to touch yourself there (she didn't yet know what the place was called), letting a boy do it to you (Maria thought this unnecessary), using the spray in the bidet (she didn't have one at home, but she would try it as soon as she visited one of her richer friends).

Anyway, once she had discovered masturbation and used a few of the techniques suggested by her friends, she abandoned forever the idea of a religious life. Masturbation gave her enormous pleasure, and yet the Church seemed to imply that sex was the greatest of sins. She heard various tales from those same girlfriends: masturbation gave you spots, could lead to madness or even pregnancy. Nevertheless, despite all these risks, she continued to pleasure herself at least once a week, usually on Wednesdays, when her father went out to play cards with his friends.

At the same time, she grew more and more insecure in her relationships with boys, and more and more determined to leave the place where she lived. She fell in love a third time and a fourth, she knew how to kiss now, and when she was alone with her boyfriends, she touched them and allowed herself to be touched, but something always went wrong, and the relationship would end precisely at the moment when she was sure that this was the person with whom she wanted to spend the rest of her life. After a long time, she came to the conclusion that men brought only pain, frustration, suffering and a sense of time dragging. One afternoon, watching a mother playing with her two-year-old son, she decided that she could still think about a husband, children and a house with a sea-view, but that she would never fall in love again, because love spoiled everything.

And so Maria's adolescent years passed. She grew prettier and prettier, and her sad, mysterious air brought her many suitors. She went out with one boy and with another, and she dreamed and suffered – despite her promise to herself never to fall in love again. On one such date, she lost her virginity on the back seat of a car; she and her boyfriend were touching each other with more than usual ardour, the boy got very worked up, and she, weary of being the only virgin amongst her group of friends, allowed him to penetrate her. Unlike masturbation, which took her up to heaven, this hurt her and caused a trickle of blood which left a stain on her skirt that took ages to wash out. There wasn't the magical sensation of her first kiss – the herons flying, the sunset, the music ... but she would rather not think about that.

She made love with the same boy a few more times, although she had to threaten him first, saying that if he didn't, she would tell her father he had raped her. She used him as a way of learning, trying in every way she could to understand what pleasure there was in having sex with a partner.

She couldn't understand it; masturbation was much less trouble and far more rewarding. But all the magazines, the TV programmes, books, girlfriends, everything, ABSOLUTELY EVERYTHING, said that a man was essential. Maria began to think that she must have some unspeakable sexual problem, so she concentrated still more on her studies and, for a while, forgot about that marvellous, murderous thing called Love.

From Maria's diary, when she was seventeen:

My aim is to understand love. I know how alive I felt when I was in love, and I know that everything I have now, however interesting it might seem, doesn't really excite me.

But love is a terrible thing: I've seen my girlfriends suffer and I don't want the same thing to happen to me. They used to laugh at me and my innocence, but now they ask me how it is I manage men so well. I smile and say nothing, because I know that the remedy is worse than the pain: I simply don't fall in love. With each day that passes, I see more clearly how fragile men are, how inconstant, insecure and surprising they are ... a few of my girlfriends' fathers have propositioned me, but I've always refused. At first, I was shocked, but now I think it's just the way men are.

Although my aim is to understand love, and although I suffer to think of the people to whom I gave my heart, I see that those who touched my heart failed to arouse my body, and that those who aroused my body failed to touch my heart.

She turned nineteen, having finished secondary school, and found a job in a draper's shop, where her boss promptly fell in love with her. By then, however, Maria knew how to use a man, without being used by him. She never let him touch her, although she was always very coquettish, conscious of the power of her beauty.

The power of beauty: what must the world be like for ugly women? She had some girlfriends who no one ever noticed at parties or who men were never interested in. Incredible though it might seem, these girls placed far greater value on the little love they received, suffered in silence when they were rejected and tried to face the future by looking for other things beyond getting all dressed up for someone else. They were more independent, took more interest in themselves, although, in Maria's imagination, the world for them must seem unbearable.

She knew how attractive she was, and although she rarely listened to her mother, there was one thing her mother said that she never forgot: 'Beauty, my dear, doesn't last.' With this in mind, she continued to keep her boss at arm's length, though without putting him off completely, and this brought her a considerable increase in salary (she didn't know how long she would be able to string him along with the mere hope of one day getting her into bed, but at least she was earning good money meanwhile). He also paid her overtime for working late (her boss liked having her around, perhaps worried that if she went out at night, she might find the great love of her life). She worked for two years solidly, paid money each month to her parents for her keep, and, at last, she did it! She saved up enough money to go and spend a week's holiday in the city of her dreams, the place where film and TV stars live, the picture postcard image of her country: Rio de Janeiro!

Her boss offered to go with her and to pay all her expenses, but Maria lied to him, saying that, since she was going to one of the most dangerous places in the world, the one condition her mother had laid down was that she was to stay at the house of a cousin trained in judo.

'Besides, sir,' she said, 'you can't just leave the shop without some reliable person to look after it.'

'Don't call me "sir",' he said, and Maria saw in his eyes something she recognised: the flame of love. And this surprised her, because she had always thought he was only interested in sex; and yet, his eyes were saying the exact opposite: 'I can give you a house, a family, some money for your parents.' Thinking of the future, she decided to stoke the fire.

She said that she would really miss the job, as well as the colleagues she just adored working with (she was careful not to mention anyone in particular, leaving the mystery hanging in the air: did 'colleague' mean him?) and she promised to take great care of her purse and her honour. The truth was quite different: she didn't want anyone, anyone at all, to spoil what would be her first week of total freedom. She wanted to do everything – swim in the sea, talk to complete strangers, look in shop windows, and be prepared for a Prince Charming to appear and carry her off for good.

'What's a week after all?' she said with a seductive smile, hoping that she was wrong. 'It will pass in a flash, and I'll soon be back at work.'

Saddened, her boss resisted at first, but finally accepted her decision, for at the time he was making secret plans to ask her to marry him as soon as she got back, and he didn't want to spoil everything by appearing too pushy.

Maria travelled for forty-eight hours by bus, checked into a cheap hotel in Copacabana (Copacabana! That beach, that sky ...) and even before she had unpacked her bags, she grabbed the bikini she had bought, put it on, and despite the cloudy weather, made straight for the beach. She looked at the sea fearfully, but ended up wading awkwardly into its waters.

No one on the beach noticed that this was her first contact with the ocean, with the goddess Iemanjá, the maritime currents, the foaming waves and, on the other side of the Atlantic, with the coast of Africa and its lions. When she came out of the water, she was approached by a woman trying to selling wholefood sandwiches, by a handsome black man who asked if she wanted to go out with him that night, and by another man who didn't speak a word of Portuguese but who asked, using gestures, if she would like to have a drink of coconut water.

Maria bought a sandwich because she was too embarrassed to say 'no', but she avoided speaking to the two strangers. She felt suddenly disappointed with herself; now that she had the chance to do anything she wanted, why was she behaving in this ridiculous manner? Finding no good explanation, she sat down to wait for the sun to come out from behind the clouds, still surprised at her own courage and at how cold the water was, even in the height of summer.

However, the man who couldn't speak Portuguese reappeared at her side bearing a drink, which he offered to her. Relieved not to have to talk to him, she drank the coconut water and smiled at him, and he smiled back. For some time, they kept up this comfortable, meaningless conversation – a smile here, a smile there – until the man took a small red dictionary out of his pocket and said, in a strange accent: 'bonita' – 'pretty'. She smiled again; however much she wanted to meet her Prince Charming, he should at least speak her language and be slightly younger.

The man went on leafing through the little book:

'Supper ... tonight?'

Then he said:

'Switzerland!'

And he completed this with words that sound like the bells of paradise in whatever language they are spoken:

'Work! Dollars!'

María did not know any restaurant called Switzerland, and could things really be that easy and dreams so quickly fulfilled? She erred on the side of caution: 'Thank you very much for the invitation, but I already have a job and I'm not interested in buying any dollars.'

The man, who understood not a word she said, was growing desperate; after many more smiles back and forth, he left her for a few minutes and returned with an interpreter. Through him, he explained that he was from Switzerland (the country, not a restaurant) and that he would like to have supper with her, in order to talk to her about a possible job offer. The interpreter, who introduced himself as the person in charge of foreign tourists and security in the hotel where the man was staying, added on his own account:

'I'd accept if I were you. He's an important impresario looking for new talent to work in Europe. If you like, I can put you in touch with some other people who accepted his invitation, got rich and are now married with children who won't have to worry about being mugged or unemployed.'

Then, trying to impress her with his grasp of international culture, he said:

'Besides, Switzerland makes excellent chocolates and watches.'

Maria's only stage experience had been in the Passion play that the local council always put on during Holy Week, and in which she had had a walk-on part as a waterseller. She had barely slept on the bus, but she was excited by the sea, tired of eating sandwiches, wholefood or otherwise, and confused because she didn't know anyone and needed to find a friend. She had been in similar situations before, in which a man promises everything and gives nothing, so she knew that all this talk of acting was just a way of getting her interested.

However, convinced that the Virgin had presented her with this chance, convinced that she must enjoy every second of her week's holiday, and because a visit to a good restaurant would provide her with something to talk about when she went home, she decided to accept the invitation, as long as the interpreter came too, for she was already getting tired of smiling and pretending that she could understand what the foreigner was saying.

The only problem was also the gravest one: she did not have anything suitable to wear. A woman never admits to such things (she would find it easier to admit that her husband had betrayed her than to reveal the state of her wardrobe), but since she did not know these people and might well never see them again, she felt that she had nothing to lose.

'I've just arrived from the northeast and I haven't got the right clothes to wear to a restaurant.'

Through the interpreter, the man told her not to worry and asked for the address of her hotel. That evening, she received a dress the like of which she had never seen in her entire life, accompanied by a pair of shoes that must have cost as much as she earned in a year.

She felt that this was the beginning of the road she had so longed for during her childhood and adolescence in the *sertão*, the Brazilian backlands, putting up with the constant droughts, the boys with no future, the poor but honest town, the dull, repetitive way of life: she was ready to be transformed into the princess of the universe! A man had offered her work, dollars, a pair of exorbitantly expensive shoes and a dress straight out of a fairy tale! All she lacked was some make-up, but the receptionist at her hotel took pity on her and helped her out, first warning her not to assume that every foreigner was trustworthy or that every man in Rio was a mugger.

Maria ignored the warning, put on her gifts from heaven, spent hours in front of the mirror, regretting not having brought a camera with her in order to record the moment,

22

only to realise that she was late for her date. She raced off, just like Cinderella, to the hotel were the Swiss gentleman was staying.

To her surprise, the interpreter told her that he would not be accompanying them.

'Don't worry about the language, what matters is whether or not he feels comfortable with you.'

'But how can he if he doesn't understand what I'm saying?'

'Precisely. You don't need to talk, it's all a question of vibes.'

Maria didn't know what 'vibes' were; where she came from, people needed to exchange words, phrases, questions and answers whenever they met. But Maílson – the name of the interpreter-cum-security officer – assured her that in Rio de Janeiro and the rest of the world, things were different.

'He doesn't need to understand, just make him feel at ease. He's a widower with no children; he owns a nightclub and is looking for Brazilian women who want to work abroad. I said you weren't the type, but he insisted, saying that he had fallen in love with you when he saw you coming out of the water. He thought your bikini was lovely too.'

He paused.

'But, frankly, if you want to find a boyfriend here, you'll have to get a different bikini; no one, apart from this Swiss guy, will go for it; it's really old-fashioned.'

Maria pretended that she hadn't heard. Maílson went on:

'I don't think he's interested in just having a bit of a fling; he reckons you've got what it takes to become the main attraction at his club. Of course, he hasn't seen you sing or dance, but you could learn all that, whereas beauty is something you're born with. These Europeans are all the same; they come over here and imagine that all Brazilian women are really sensual and know how to samba. If he's serious, I'd advise you to get a signed contract and have the signature verified at the Swiss consulate before leaving the country. I'll be on the beach tomorrow, opposite the hotel, if you want to talk to me about anything.'

The Swiss man, all smiles, took her arm and indicated the taxi awaiting them.

'If he has other intentions, and you have too, then the normal price is three hundred dollars a night. Don't accept any less.'

Before she could say anything, she was on her way to the restaurant, with the man rehearsing the words he wanted to say. The conversation was very simple:

'Work? Dollars? Brazilian star?'

Maria, meanwhile, was still thinking about what the interpreter-cum-security officer had said: three hundred dollars a night! That was a fortune! She didn't need to suffer for love, she could play this man along just as she had her boss at the shop, get married, have children and give her parents a comfortable life. What did she have to lose? He was old and he might die before too long, and then she would be rich – these Swiss men obviously had too much money and not enough women back home.

They said little over the meal – just the usual exchange of smiles – and Maria gradually began to understand what Maílson had meant by 'vibes'. The man showed her an

24

album containing writing in a language that she did not know; photos of women in bikinis (doubtless better and more daring than the one she had worn that afternoon), newspaper cuttings, garish leaflets in which the only word she recognised was 'Brazil', wrongly spelled (hadn't they taught him at school that it was written with an 's'?). She drank a lot, afraid that the man would proposition her (after all, even though she had never done this in her life before, no one could turn their nose up at three hundred dollars, and things always seem simpler with a bit of alcohol inside you, especially if you're among strangers). But the man behaved like a perfect gentleman, even holding her chair for her when she sat down and got up. In the end, she said that she was tired and arranged to meet him on the beach the following day (pointing to her watch, showing him the time, making the movement of the waves with her hands and saying 'a-ma-nhã' – 'tomorrow' – very slowly).

He seemed pleased and looked at his own watch (possibly Swiss), and agreed on the time.

She did not go to sleep straight away. She dreamed that it was all a dream. Then she woke up and saw that it wasn't: there was the dress draped over the chair in her modest room, the beautiful shoes and that rendezvous on the beach.

From Maria's diary, on the day that she met the Swiss man:

Everything tells me that I am about to make a wrong decision, but making mistakes is just part of life. What does the world want of me? Does it want me to take no risks, to go back where I came from because I didn't have the courage to say 'yes' to life?

I made my first mistake when I was eleven years old, when that boy asked me if I could lend him a pencil; since then, I've realised that sometimes you get no second chance and that it's best to accept the gifts the world offers you. Of course it's risky, but is the risk any greater than the chance of the bus that took forty-eight hours to bring me here having an accident? If I must be faithful to someone or something, then I have, first of all, to be faithful to myself. If I'm looking for true love, I first have to get the mediocre loves out of my system. The little experience of life I've had has taught me that no one owns anything, that everything is an illusion – and that applies to material as well as spiritual things. Anyone who has lost something they thought was theirs forever (as has happened often enough to me already) finally comes to realise that nothing really belongs to them.

And if nothing belongs to me, then there's no point wasting my time looking after things that aren't mine; it's best to live as if today were the first (or last) day of my life.

The next day, together with Maílson, the interpreter-cum-security officer and now, according to him, her agent, she said that she would accept the Swiss man's offer, as long as she had a document provided by the Swiss consulate. The foreigner, who seemed accustomed to such demands, said that this was something he wanted too, since, if she was to work in his country, she needed a piece of paper proving that no one there could do the job she was proposing to do – and this was not particularly difficult, given that Swiss women had no particular talent for the samba. Together they went to the city centre, and the security officer-cum-interpreter-cum-agent demanded a cash advance as soon as the contract was signed, thirty per cent of the five hundred dollars she received.

'That's a week's payment in advance. One week, you understand? You'll be earning five hundred dollars a week from now on, but with no deductions, because I only get a commission on the first payment.'

Up until then, travel and the idea of going far away had just been a dream, and dreaming is very pleasant as long as you are not forced to put your dreams into practice. That way, we avoid all the risks, frustrations and difficulties, and when we are old, we can always blame other people – preferably our parents, our spouses or our children – for our failure to realise our dreams.

Suddenly, there was the opportunity she had been so eagerly awaiting, but which she had hoped would never come! How could she possibly deal with the challenges and the dangers of a life she did not know? How could she leave behind everything she was used to? Why had the Virgin decided to go this far?

Maria consoled herself with the thought that she could change her mind at any moment; it was all just a silly game, something different to tell her friends about when she went back home. After all, she lived more than a thousand kilometres from there and she now had three hundred and fifty dollars in her purse, so if, tomorrow, she decided to pack her bags and run away, there was no way they would ever be able to track her down again.

In the afternoon following their visit to the consulate, she decided to go for a walk on her own by the sea, where she looked at the children, the volleyball players, the beggars, the drunks, the sellers of traditional Brazilian artifacts (made in China), the people jogging and exercising as a way of fending off old age, the foreign tourists, the mothers with their children, and the pensioners playing cards at the far end of the promenade. She had come to Rio de Janeiro, she had been to a five-star restaurant and to a consulate, she had met a foreigner, she had an agent, she had been given a present of a dress and a pair of shoes that no one, absolutely no one, back home could ever have afforded.

And now what?

She looked out to sea: her geography lessons told her that if she set off in a straight line, she would reach Africa, with its lions and jungles full of gorillas. However, if she headed in a slightly more northerly direction, she would end up in the enchanted kingdom known as Europe, with its Eiffel Tower, EuroDisney and Leaning Tower of Pizza. What did she have to lose? Like every Brazilian girl, she had learned to samba even before she could say 'Mama'; she could always come back if she didn't like it, and she had already learned that opportunities are made to be seized.

She had spent a lot of her life saying 'no' to things to which she would have liked to say 'yes', determined to try only those experiences she could control – certain affairs she had had with men, for example. Now she was facing the unknown, as unknown as this sea had once been to the navigators who crossed it, or so she had been told in history classes. She could always say 'no', but would she then spend the rest of her life brooding over it, as she still did over the memory of the little boy who had once asked to borrow a pencil and had then disappeared – her first love? She could always say 'no', but why not try saying 'yes' this time?

For one very simple reason: she was a girl from the backlands of Brazil, with no experience of life apart from a good school, a vast knowledge of TV soaps and the certainty that she was beautiful. That wasn't enough with which to face the world.

She saw a group of people laughing and looking at the sea, afraid to go in. Two days ago, she had felt the same thing, but now she was no longer afraid; she went into the water whenever she wanted, as if she had been born there. Wouldn't it be the same in Europe?

29

She made a silent prayer and again asked the Virgin Mary's advice, and seconds later, she seemed perfectly at ease with her decision to go ahead, because she felt protected. She could always come back, but she would not necessarily get another chance of a trip like this. It was worth taking the risk, as long as the dream survived the forty-eight-hour journey back home in a bus with no air conditioning, and as long as the Swiss man didn't change his mind.

She was in such good spirits that when he invited her out to supper again, she wanted to appear alluring and took his hand in hers, but he immediately pulled away, and Maria realised – with a mixture of fear and relief – that he was serious about what he said.

'Samba star!' said the man. 'Lovely Brazilian samba star! Travel next week!'

This was all well and good, but 'travel next week' was out of the question. Maria explained that she couldn't take a decision without first consulting her family. The Swiss man was furious and showed her a copy of the signed contract, and for the first time she felt afraid.

'Contract!' he said.

Even though she was determined to go home, she decided to consult her agent Maílson first; after all, he was being paid to advise her.

Maílson, however, seemed more concerned with seducing a German tourist who had just arrived at the hotel and who was sunbathing topless on the beach, convinced that Brazil was the most liberal country in the world (having failed to notice that she was the only woman on the beach with her breasts exposed and that everyone was eyeing her rather uneasily). It was very hard to get him to pay attention to what she was saying.

'But what if I change my mind?' insisted Maria.

'I don't know what's in the contract, but I suppose he might have you arrested.'

'He'd never be able to find me!'

'Exactly. So why worry?'

The Swiss man, on the other hand, having spent five hundred dollars, as well as paying out for a pair of shoes, a dress, two suppers and various fees for the paperwork at the consulate, was beginning to get worried, and so, since Maria kept insisting on the need to talk to her family, he decided to buy two plane tickets and go with her to the place where she had been born – as long as it could all be resolved in forty-eight hours and they could still travel to Europe the following week, as agreed. With a smile here and a smile there, she was beginning to understand that this was all in the documents she had signed and that, when it came to seductions, feelings and contracts, one should never play around.

It was a surprise and a source of pride to the small town to see its lovely daughter Maria arrive accompanied by a foreigner who wanted to make her a big star in Europe. The whole neighbourhood knew, and her old schoolfriends asked: 'How did it happen?'

'I was just lucky.'

They wanted to know if such things were always happening in Rio de Janeiro, because they had seen similar scenarios in TV soaps. Maria would not be pinned down, wanting to place a high value on her personal experience and thus convince her friends that she was someone special.

She and the man went to her house where he handed round leaflets, with Brasil spelled with a 'z', and the contract, while Maria explained that she had an agent 'now and intended following a career as an actress. Her mother, seeing the diminutive bikinis worn by the girls in the photos that the foreigner was showing her, immediately gave them back and preferred to ask no questions; all that mattered was that her daughter should be happy and rich, or unhappy, but at least rich.

'What's his name?'

'Roger.'

'Rogério! I had a cousin called Rogério!'

The man smiled and clapped, and they all realised that he hadn't understood a word. Maria's father said:

'He's about the same age as me.'

Her mother told him not to interfere with their daughter's happiness. Since all seamstresses talk a great deal to their customers and acquire a great deal of knowledge about marriage and love, her advice to Maria was this:

'My dear, it's better to be unhappy with a rich man than happy with a poor man, and over there you'll have far more chance of becoming an unhappy rich woman. Besides, if it doesn't work out, you can just get on the bus and come home.'

Maria might be a girl from the backlands, but she was more intelligent than her mother or her future husband imagined, and she said, simply to be provocative:

'Mama, there isn't a bus from Europe to Brazil. Besides, I want a career as a performer, I'm not looking for marriage.'

Her mother gave her a look of near despair.

'If you can go there, you can always come back. Being a performer, an actress, is fine for a young woman, but it only lasts as long as your looks, and they start to fade when you're about thirty. So make the most of things now. Find someone who's honest and loving, and marry him. Love isn't that important. I didn't love your father at first, but money buys everything, even true love. And look at your father, he's not even rich!'

It was bad advice from a friend, but good advice from a mother. Forty-eight hours later, Maria was back in Rio, though not without first having made a visit, alone, to her old place of work in order to hand in her resignation and to hear the owner of the shop say:

'Yes, I'd heard that a big French impresario wanted to take you off to Paris. I can't stop you going in pursuit of your happiness, but I want you to know something before you leave.'

He took a medal on a chain out of his pocket.

'It's the Miraculous Medal of Our Lady of the Graces. She has a church in Paris, so go there and pray for her protection. Look, there are some words engraved around the Virgin.'

Maria read: 'Hail Mary conceived without sin, pray for us who turn to you. Amen.'

'Remember to say those words at least once a day. And ...'

He hesitated, but it was getting late.

'... if one day you come back, I'll be waiting for you. I missed my chance to tell you something very simple: I love you. It may be too late now, but I wanted you to know.'

Missed chances. She had learned very early on what that meant. 'I love you', though, were three words she had often heard during her twenty-two years, and it seemed to her that they were now completely devoid of meaning, because they had never turned into anything serious or deep, never translated into a lasting relationship. Maria thanked him for his words, noted them in her memory (one never knows what life may have in store for us, and it's always good to know where the emergency exit is), gave him a chaste kiss on the cheek and left without so much as a backward glance.

They returned to Rio, and within a day she had her passport (Brazil had really changed, Roger said, using a few words in Portuguese and a lot of gestures, which Maria took to mean 'before it used to take ages'). With the help of Maílson, the security officer-cum-interpreter-cum-agent, any other important purchases were made (clothes, shoes, make-up, everything that a woman like her could want). On the eve of their departure for Europe, they went to a nightclub, and when Roger saw her dance, he felt pleased with his choice; he was clearly in the presence of a future great star of Cabaret Cologny, this lovely dark girl with her pale eyes and hair as black as the wing of the *graúna* (the Brazilian bird often evoked by local authors to describe black hair). The work permit from the Swiss consulate was ready, so they packed their bags and, the following day, they were flying to the land of chocolate, clocks and cheese, with Maria secretly planning to make this man fall in love with her – after all, he wasn't old, ugly or poor. What more could she want?

She arrived feeling exhausted and, while still in the airport, her heart contracted with fear: she realised that she was completely dependent on the man at her side – she had no knowledge of the country, the language or the cold. Roger's behaviour changed as the hours passed; he no longer made any attempt to be pleasant, and although he had never tried to kiss her or to fondle her breasts, the look in his eyes grew more and more distant. He installed her in a small hotel, introducing her to another young Brazilian woman, a sad creature called Vivian, who would be in charge of preparing her for the work.

Vivian looked her coolly up and down, without the least show of sympathy for someone who had clearly never been abroad before. Instead of asking her how she was feeling, she got straight down to business.

'Don't delude yourself. He flies off to Brazil whenever one of his dancers gets married, something which seems to be happening more and more frequently. He knows what you want, and I assume you do too: you're probably looking for one of three things – adventure, money or a husband.'

How did she know? Was everyone looking for the same thing? Or could Vivian read other people's thoughts?

'All the girls here are looking for one of those three things,' Vivian went on, and Maria was convinced that she really could read her thoughts. 'As for adventure, it's too cold to do anything and, besides, you won't earn enough to go off travelling. And as for money, once the cost of room and board has been deducted, you'll have to work for nearly a whole year just to pay for your flight back home.'

'But ...'

'I know, that isn't what you agreed. But the truth is that, like everyone else, you forgot to ask. If you had been more careful, if you had read the contract you signed, you would know exactly what you were getting yourself into, because the Swiss don't lie, they just rely on silence to help them.'

Maria felt the ground shifting beneath her.

'And as for a husband, every time a girl gets married, that represents a great financial loss for Roger, so we're forbidden to talk to the customers. If your interests lie in that direction, you'll have to run great risks. This isn't a pick-up place, like in Rue de Berne.'

Rue de Berne?

'Men come here with their wives, and the few tourists who turn up get one whiff of the family atmosphere and go looking for women elsewhere. I presume you know how to dance; well, if you can sing as well, your salary will increase, but so will the other girls' envy, so I'd suggest that, even if you're the best singer in Brazil, forget all about it and don't even try. Above all, don't use the phone. You'll spend everything you earn on it, and that won't be much.'

'He promised me five hundred dollars a week!'

'Oh yeah.'

From Maria's diary, during her second week in Switzerland:

I went to the nightclub and met the dance director who comes from somewhere called Morocco, and I had to learn every step of what he – who has never set foot in Brazil – thinks is the samba. I didn't even have time to recover from the long flight, I had to start smiling and dancing on the very first night. There are six of us, and not one of us is happy and none of us knows what we're doing here. The customers drink and applaud, blow kisses and privately make obscene gestures, but that's as far as it goes.

I got paid yesterday, barely a tenth of what we agreed, the rest, according to the contract, will be used to pay for my flight and my stay here. According to Vivian's calculations, that will take a year, which means that during that time there's no escape.

And what's the point of escaping anyway? I've only just arrived. I haven't seen anything yet. What's so awful about having to dance seven nights a week? I used to do that for pleasure, now I do it for money and fame; my legs don't ache, the only difficult thing is maintaining that fixed smile.

I can choose either to be a victim of the world or an adventurer in search of treasure. It's all a question of how I view my life.

Maria chose to be an adventurer in search of treasure – she put aside her feelings, she stopped crying every night, and she forgot all about the person she used to be; she discovered that she had enough willpower to pretend that she had just been born and so had no reason to miss anyone. Feelings could wait, now what she needed to do was to earn some money, get to know the country and return home victorious.

Besides, everything around her was very like Brazil in general and her own small town in particular: the women spoke Portuguese, complained about men, talked loudly, moaned about their working hours, turned up late at the club, defied the boss, thought themselves the most beautiful women in the world, and told stories about their Prince Charmings, who were usually living miles away or were married or had no money and so sponged off them. Contrary to what she had imagined from the leaflets Roger had brought with him, the club was exactly as Vivian had said it was: it had a family atmosphere. The girls – described on their work permits as 'samba dancers' – were not allowed to accept invitations or to go out with the customers. If they were caught receiving a note with someone's telephone number on it, they were suspended from work for two whole weeks. Maria, who had expected something livelier and more exciting, gradually allowed herself to succumb to sadness and boredom.

During the first two weeks, she barely left the boarding house where she was living, especially when she discovered that no one spoke her language, even if she said everything VE-RY SLOW-LY. She was also surprised to learn that, unlike in her own country, the city in which she was living had two different names – it was Genève to those who lived there and Genebra to Brazilians.

Finally, in the long, tedious hours spent in her small, TV-less room, she concluded:

(a) she would never find what she was looking for if she couldn't express herself. In order to do that, she needed to learn the local language.

(b) since all her colleagues were looking for the same thing, she needed to be different. For that particular problem, she as yet lacked both a solution or a method.

From Maria's diary, four weeks after arriving in Genève/Genebra:

I've already been here an eternity, I don't speak the language, I spend all day listening to music on the radio, looking round my room, thinking about Brazil, longing for work to begin and, when I'm working, longing to get back to the boarding house. In other words, I'm living the future not the present.

One day, at some distant future date, I'll get my ticket home, and I can go back to Brazil, marry the owner of the draper's shop and listen to the malicious comments of those friends who, never having taken any risks themselves, can only see other people's failures. No, I can't go back like that. I'd rather throw myself out of the plane as it's crossing the ocean.

Since you can't open the windows in the plane (I had never expected that. What a shame not to be able to breathe in the pure air!), I will die here. But before I die, I want to fight for life. If I can walk on my own, I can go wherever I like.

The following day, she enrolled in a French course that was run in the mornings, and there she met people of all creeds, beliefs and ages, men wearing brightly coloured clothes and lots of gold bracelets, women who always wore a headscarf, children who learned more quickly than the grown-ups, when it should have been the other way round, since grown-ups have more experience. She felt proud when she found out that everyone knew about her country – Carnival, the samba, football, and the most famous person in the world, Pelê. At first, she wanted to be nice and so tried to correct their pronunciation (it's Pelê! Pelê!), but after a while, she gave up, since they also insisted on calling her Maria, with that mania foreigners have for changing all foreign names and believing that they are always right.

In the afternoons, so as to practise the language, she took her first steps around this city of two names. She discovered some delicious chocolate, a cheese she had never eaten before, a huge fountain in the middle of the lake, snow (which no one back home had ever touched), storks, and restaurants with fireplaces (although she never went inside, just seeing the fire blazing away gave her a pleasant feeling of wellbeing). She was also surprised to find that not all the shop signs advertised clocks; there were banks too, although she couldn't quite understand why there were so many for so few inhabitants, and why she rarely saw anyone inside them. She decided, however, not to ask any questions.

After three months of keeping a tight rein on herself at work, her Brazilian blood – as sensual and sexual as everyone thinks – made its voice heard; she fell in love with an Arab who was studying French with her on the same course. The affair lasted three weeks until, one night, she decided to take time off and go and visit a mountain on the outskirts of Geneva; this provoked a summons to Roger's office as soon as she arrived at work the following day.

No sooner had she opened the door than she was summarily dismissed for setting a bad example to the other girls working there. A hysterical Roger said that, yet again, he had been let down, that Brazilian women couldn't be trusted (oh dear, this mania for making generalisations about everything). She tried telling him that she had had a very high fever brought on by the sudden change in climate, but the man would not be persuaded and even claimed that he would have to go straight back to Brazil in order to find a replacement, and that he would have been far better off putting on a show using Yugoslav music and Yugoslav dancers who were far prettier and far more reliable.

Maria might be young but she was no fool, especially once her Arab lover had told her that Swiss employment laws were very strict and, since the nightclub kept back a large part of her salary, she could easily allege that she was being used for slave labour.

She went back to Roger's office, this time speaking reasonable French, which now included the word 'lawyer'. She left with a few insults and five thousand dollars in compensation – a sum of money beyond her wildest dreams – and all because of that magic word 'lawyer'. Now she was free to spend time with her Arab lover, buy a few presents, take some photos of the snow, and go back home in triumph.

The first thing she did was telephone her mother's neighbour to say that she was happy, had a brilliant career ahead of her and that there was no need for her family to worry. Then, since she had to leave the room in the boarding house that Roger had arranged for her, she had no alternative but to go to her Arab boyfriend, swear undying love, convert to his religion and marry him, even if she had to wear one of those strange headscarves; after all, as everyone knew, all Arabs were extremely wealthy and that was enough.

The Arab, however, was already far away, possibly in Arabia, a country Maria had never even heard of, and, deep down, she gave thanks to the Virgin Mary because she had not been obliged to betray her religion. She now had a reasonable grasp of spoken French, enough money for her return ticket, a work permit as a 'samba dancer' and a current visa; so, knowing that she could always go back and marry her former boss, she decided to try to earn money with her looks.

In Brazil she had read a book about a shepherd who, in searching for his treasure, encounters various difficulties, and these difficulties help him to get what he wants; she was in exactly the same position. She was aware now that the reason she had been dismissed was so that she could find her true destiny, as a model.

She rented a small room (with no television, but she had to live frugally until she began earning lots of money), and the following day, started doing the rounds of the agencies.

They all told her that she needed to get some professional photos taken, but this, after all, was an investment in her career – dreams don't come cheap. She spent a large part of her money on an excellent photographer, who spoke little, but was extremely demanding: he had a vast selection of clothes in his studio and she posed for him in various outfits, sober and extravagant, and even in a bikini of which the only person she knew in Rio de Janeiro, the security officer-cum-interpreter-cum-former agent, Maílson, would have been proud. She asked for several extra copies and sent them off to her family with a letter saying how happy she was in Switzerland. They would all think she was rich and the owner of an enviable wardrobe, and that she had been transformed into her town's most illustrious daughter. If all went to plan (and she had read enough books on 'positive thinking' to be convinced that victory was assured), she would be greeted by a brass band on her return home and would try to persuade the mayor to have a square named after her.

Since she had no permanent address, she bought a mobile phone, the sort that use pre-paid phone cards, and in the days that followed, she waited for job offers. She ate in Chinese restaurants (which were the cheapest) and, to pass the time, she studied furiously.

But time dragged, and the telephone didn't ring. To her surprise, no one bothered her when she went for walks by the lake, apart from a few drug-pushers who always hung around in the same place, underneath one of the bridges that connect the lovely old public gardens to the newer part of the city. She began to doubt her looks, until an ex-colleague, whom she bumped into by chance in a café, told her that it wasn't her fault, it was the fault of the Swiss, who hate to bother anyone, and of other foreigners, who were all afraid of being arrested for 'sexual harassment' – a concept invented to make women everywhere feel worse about themselves.

From Maria's diary, one night when she lacked the courage to go out, to live or to continue waiting for the phone call that never came:

> *I spent today outside a funfair. Since I can't afford to fritter my money away, I thought it best just to watch other people. I stood for a long time by the roller coaster, and I noticed that most people get on it in search of excitement, but that once it starts, they are terrified and want the cars to stop.*
>
> *What do they expect? Having chosen adventure, shouldn't they be prepared to go the whole way? Or do they think that the intelligent thing to do would be to avoid the ups and downs and spend all their time on a carousel, going round and round on the spot?*
>
> *At the moment, I'm far too lonely to think about love, but I have to believe that it will happen, that I will find a job and that I am here because I chose this fate. The roller coaster is my life; life is a fast, dizzying game; life is a parachute jump; it's taking chances, falling over and getting up again; it's mountaineering; it's wanting to get to the very top of yourself and to feel angry and dissatisfied when you don't manage it.*
>
> *It isn't easy being far from my family and from the language in which I can express all my feelings and*

emotions, but, from now on, whenever I feel depressed, I will remember that funfair. If I had fallen asleep and suddenly woken up on a roller coaster, what would I feel?

Well, I would feel trapped and sick, terrified of every bend, wanting to get off. However, if I believe that the track is my destiny and that God is in charge of the machine, then the nightmare becomes something thrilling. It becomes exactly what it is, a roller coaster, a safe, reliable toy, which will eventually stop, but, while the journey lasts, I must look at the surrounding landscape and whoop with excitement.

Although she was capable of writing very wise thoughts, she was quite incapable of following her own advice; her periods of depression became more frequent and the phone still refused to ring. To distract herself during these empty hours, and in order to practise her French, she began buying magazines about celebrities, but realised at once that she was spending too much money, and so she looked for the nearest lending library. The woman in charge told her that they didn't lend out magazines, but that she could suggest a few books that would help improve her French.

'I haven't got time to read books.'

'What do you mean you haven't got time? What are you doing?'

'Lots of things: studying French, writing a diary, and ...'

'And what?'

She was about to say 'waiting for the phone to ring', but she thought it best to say nothing.

'My dear, you're still very young, you've got your whole life ahead of you. Read. Forget everything you've been told about books and just read.'

'I've read loads of books.'

Suddenly, Maria remembered what Maílson the security officer had told her about 'vibes'. The librarian before her seemed a very sweet, sensitive person, someone who might be able to help her if all else failed. She needed to win her over;

her instinct was telling her that this woman could become her friend. She quickly changed tack.

'But I'd like to read more. Could you help me choose some books?'

The woman brought her *The Little Prince*. She started leafing through it that same night, saw the drawings on the first page of what seemed to be a hat, but which, according to the author, all children would instantly recognise as a snake with an elephant inside it. 'Well, I don't think I can ever have been a child, then,' she thought. 'To me, it looks more like a hat.' In the absence of any television to watch, she accompanied the prince on his journeys, feeling sad whenever the word 'love' appeared, for she had forbidden herself to think about the subject at the risk of feeling suicidal. However, apart from the painful, romantic scenes between a prince, a fox and a rose, the book was really interesting, and she didn't keep checking every five minutes that the battery in her mobile phone was still fully charged (she was terrified of missing her big chance purely out of carelessness).

Maria became a regular visitor to the library, where she would chat to the woman, who seemed as lonely as she was, ask her to suggest more books and discuss life and authors – until her money had nearly run out. Another two weeks and she would not even have enough left to buy her ticket back to Brazil.

And, since life always waits for some crisis to occur before revealing itself at its most brilliant, the phone finally rang.

Three months after discovering the word 'lawyer' and after two months of living on the compensation she had received, someone from a model agency asked if Senhora Maria was still at this number. The reply was a cool, long-rehearsed 'yes', so as not to appear too eager. She learned that an Arab gentleman, who worked in the fashion industry in his country, had been very taken by her photos and wanted to invite her to take part in a fashion show. Maria remembered her recent disappointments, but also the money that she so desperately needed.

They arranged to meet in a very chic restaurant. She found herself with an elegant man, older and more charming than Roger, who asked her:

'Do you know who painted that picture over there? It's a Miró. Have you heard of Joan Miró?'

Maria said nothing, as if she were concentrating on the food, rather different from that in the Chinese restaurants where she normally ate. Meanwhile, she made a mental note: on her next visit to the library, she would have to ask for a book about Miró.

But the Arab was saying:

'This was the table where Fellini always sat. Do you know his films at all?'

She said she adored them. The man began asking more probing questions and Maria, knowing that she would fail the test, decided to be straight with him:

'I'm not going to spend the evening pretending to you. I can just about tell the difference between Coca-Cola and Pepsi, but that's about it. I thought we came here to discuss a fashion show.'

He seemed to appreciate her frankness.

'We'll do that when we have our after-supper drink.'

There was a pause, while they looked at each other, each trying to imagine what the other was thinking.

'You're very pretty,' said the man. 'If you come up and have a drink with me in my hotel room, I'll give you a thousand francs.'

Maria understood at once. Was it the fault of the model agency? Was it her fault? Should she have found out more about the nature of this supper? It wasn't the agency's fault, or hers, or the man's: this was simply how things worked. Suddenly she missed her hometown, missed Brazil, missed her mother's arms. She remembered Maílson, on the beach, when he had mentioned a fee of three hundred dollars; at the time, she had thought it funny, much more than she would have expected to receive for spending the night with a man. However, at that moment, she realised that she had no one, absolutely no one in the world she could talk to; she was alone in a strange city, a relatively experienced twenty-two-year-old, but none of her experience could help her to decide what would be the best response.

'Could you pour me some more wine, please.'

The Arab man filled her glass, and her thoughts travelled faster than the Little Prince on his travels to all those planets. She had come in search of adventure, money and possibly a husband; she had known that she would end up getting proposals such as this, because she was no innocent and was used to the ways of men. She still believed in model agencies, stardom, a rich husband, a family, children, grandchildren, nice clothes, a triumphant return to the place where she was born. She dreamed of overcoming all difficulties purely by dint of her own intelligence, charm and willpower.

But reality had just fallen in on her. To the man's surprise, she began to cry. He did not know what to do, caught between his fear of causing a scandal and his instinctive desire to protect her. He called the waiter over in order to ask for the bill, but Maria stopped him.

'No, don't do that. Pour me some more wine and just let me cry for a while.'

And Maria thought about the little boy who had asked to borrow a pencil, about the young man who had kissed her and how she had kept her mouth closed, about her excitement at seeing Rio for the first time, about the men who had used her and given nothing back, about the passions and loves lost along the way. Despite her apparent freedom, her life consisted of endless hours spent waiting for a miracle, for true love, for an adventure with the same romantic ending she had seen in films and read about in books. A writer once said that it is not time that changes man, nor knowledge; the only thing that can change someone's mind is love. What nonsense! The person who wrote that clearly knew only one side of the coin.

Love was undoubtedly one of the things capable of changing a person's whole life, from one moment to the next. But there was the other side of the coin, the second thing that could make a human being take a totally different course from the one he or she had planned; and that was called despair. Yes, perhaps love really could transform someone, but despair did the job more quickly. What should she do? Should she run back to Brazil, become a teacher of French and marry her former boss? Should she take a small step forward; after all, it was only one night, in a city where she knew no one and no one knew her. Would that one night and that easy money mean that she would inevitably carry on until she reached a point in the road where there was no turning back? What was happening here – a great opportunity or a test set her by the Virgin Mary?

The Arab was looking around at the paintings by Joan Miró, at the place where Fellini used to have lunch, at the girl who took the coats and at the other customers arriving and leaving.

'Didn't you realise?'

'More wine, please,' said Maria, still in tears.

She was praying that the waiter would not come over and realise what was going on, and the waiter, who was watching it all from a distance, out of the corner of his eye, was praying that the man and the girl would hurry up and pay the bill, because the restaurant was full and there were people waiting.

At last, after what seemed an eternity, she spoke:

'Did you say a thousand francs for one drink?'

Maria was surprised by her own tone of voice.

'Yes,' said the man, regretting having suggested it in the first place. 'But I really wouldn't want …'

'Pay the bill and let's go and have that drink at your hotel.'

Again, she seemed like a stranger to herself. Up until then, she had been a nice, cheerful, well-brought-up girl, and she would never have spoken like that to a stranger. But that girl, it seemed to her, had died forever: before her lay another existence, in which drinks cost one thousand francs or, to use a more universal currency, about six hundred dollars.

And everything happened as expected: she went to the Arab's hotel, drank champagne, got herself almost completely drunk, opened her legs, waited for him to have an orgasm (it didn't even occur to her to pretend to have one too), washed herself in the marble bathroom, picked up the money, and allowed herself the luxury of a taxi home.

She fell into bed and slept dreamlessly all night.

From Maria's diary, the next day:

I remember everything, although not the moment when I made the decision. Oddly enough, I have no sense of guilt. I used to think of girls who went to bed with men for money as people who had no other choice, and now I see that it isn't like that. I could have said 'yes' or 'no'; no one was forcing me to accept anything.

I walk about the streets and look at all the people, and I wonder if they chose their lives? Or were they, like me, 'chosen' by fate? The housewife who dreamed of becoming a model, the banker who wanted to be a musician, the dentist who felt he should write a book and devote himself to literature, the girl who would have loved to be a TV star, but who found herself instead working at the checkout in a supermarket.

I don't feel in the least bit sorry for myself. I am still not a victim, because I could have left that restaurant with my dignity intact and my purse empty. I could have given that man sitting opposite me a lesson in morality or tried to make him see that before him

*sat a princess who should be wooed not bought. I
could have responded in all kinds of ways, but – like
most people – I let fate choose which route I should
take.*

*I'm not the only one, even though my fate may put
me outside the law and outside society. In the search
for happiness, however, we are all equal: none of us is
happy – not the banker/musician, the dentist/writer,
the checkout girl/actress, or the housewife/model.*

So that was how it worked. As easy as that. There she was in a strange city where she knew no one, but what had been a torment to her yesterday, today gave her a tremendous sense of freedom, because she didn't need to explain herself to anyone.

She decided that, for the first time in many years, she would devote the entire day to thinking about herself. Up until then, she had always been preoccupied with what other people were thinking: her mother, her schoolfriends, her father, the people at the model agencies, the French teacher, the waiter, the librarian, complete strangers in the street. In fact, no one was thinking anything, certainly not about her, a poor foreigner, who, if she disappeared tomorrow, wouldn't even be missed by the police.

Fine. She went out early, had breakfast in her usual café, went for a stroll around the lake and saw a demonstration held by refugees. A woman out walking a small dog told her that they were Kurds, and Maria, instead of pretending that she knew the answer in order to prove that she was more cultivated and intelligent than people might think, asked:

'Where do Kurds come from?'

To her surprise, the woman didn't know. That's what the world is like: people talk as if they knew everything, but if you dare to ask a question, they don't know anything. She went into an Internet café and discovered that the Kurds came from Kurdistan, a non-existent country, now divided between Turkey and Iraq. She went back to the lake in search of the woman and her dog, but she had gone, possibly because the dog had got fed up after half an hour of staring at a group of human beings with banners, headscarves, music and strange cries.

'I'm just like that woman really. Or rather, that's what I used to be like: someone pretending to know everything, hidden away in my own silence, until that Arab guy got on my nerves, and I finally had the courage to say that the only thing I knew was how to tell the difference between two soft drinks. Was he shocked? Did he change his mind about me? Of course not. He must have been amazed at my honesty. Whenever I try to appear more intelligent than I am, I always lose out. Well, enough is enough!'

She thought of the model agency. Did they know what the Arab guy really wanted – in which case she had, yet again, been taken for a fool – or had they genuinely thought he was going to find work for her in his country?

Whatever the truth of the matter, Maria felt less alone on that grey morning in Geneva, with the temperature close to zero, the Kurds demonstrating, the trams arriving punctually at each stop, the shops setting out their jewellery in the windows again, the banks opening, the beggars sleeping, the Swiss going to work. She was less alone because by her side was another woman, invisible perhaps to passersby. She had never noticed her presence before, but there she was.

She smiled at the invisible woman beside her who looked like the Virgin Mary, Jesus's mother. The woman smiled back and told her to be careful, things were not as simple as she imagined. Maria ignored the advice and replied that she was a grown-up, responsible for her own decisions, and she couldn't believe that there was some cosmic conspiracy being hatched against her. She had learned that there were people prepared to pay one thousand Swiss francs for one night, for half an hour between her legs, and all she had to decide over the next few days was whether to take her thousand Swiss francs and buy a plane ticket back to the town where she had been born, or to stay a little longer, and earn enough to be able to buy her parents a house, some lovely clothes for herself and tickets to all the places she had dreamed of visiting one day.

The invisible woman at her side said again that things weren't that simple, but Maria, although glad of this unexpected company, asked her not to interrupt her thoughts, because she needed to make some important decisions.

She began to analyse, more carefully this time, the possibility of going back to Brazil. Her schoolfriends, who had never left the town they were born in, would all say that she had been fired from the job, that she had never had the talent to be an international star. Her mother would be sad never to have received her promised monthly sum of money, although Maria, in her letters, had assured her that the post office must be stealing it. Her father would, forever after, look at her with that 'I told you so' expression on his face; she would go back to working in the shop, selling fabrics, and she would marry the owner – she who had travelled in a plane, eaten Swiss cheese, learned French and walked in the snow.

On the other hand, there were those drinks that had

earned her one thousand Swiss francs. It might not last very long – after all, beauty changes as swiftly as the wind – but in a year, she could earn enough money to get back on her feet and return to the world, this time on her own terms. The only real problem was that she didn't know what to do, how to start. She remembered from her days at the 'family night-club' where she had first worked that a girl had mentioned somewhere called Rue de Berne – in fact, it had been one of the first things she had said, even before she had shown her where to put her suitcases.

She went over to one of the large panels that can be found everywhere in Geneva, that most tourist-friendly of cities, which cannot bear to see tourists getting lost. For this reason the panels have advertisements on one side and maps on the other.

A man was standing there, and she asked him if he knew where Rue de Berne was. He looked at her, intrigued, and asked if it was the street she was looking for or the road that went to Berne, the capital of Switzerland. No, said Maria, I want the street in Geneva. The man looked her up and down, then walked off without a word, convinced that he was being filmed by one of those TV programmes that delight in making fools of people. Maria studied the map for fifteen minutes – it's not a very big city – and finally found the place she was looking for.

Her invisible friend, who had remained silent while she was studying the map, was now trying to reason with her; it wasn't a question of morality, but of setting off down a road of no return.

Maria said that if she could earn enough money to go

back home, then she could earn enough to get out of any situation. Besides, none of the people she passed had actually chosen what they wanted to do. That was just a fact of life.

'We live in a vale of tears,' she said to her invisible friend. 'We can have all the dreams we like, but life is hard, implacable, sad. What are you trying to say: that people will condemn me? No one will ever know – this is just one phase of my life.'

With a sad, sweet smile, the invisible friend disappeared.

Maria went to the funfair and bought a ticket for the roller coaster; she screamed along with everyone else, knowing that there was no real danger and that it was all just a game. She ate in a Japanese restaurant, even though she didn't understand quite what she was eating, knowing only that it was very expensive and feeling in a mood to indulge herself in every luxury. She was happy, she didn't need to wait for a phone call now or to watch every centime she spent.

Later that day, she left a message with the agency to thank them and to tell them that the meeting had gone well. If they were genuine, they would ask about the photos. If they were procurers of women, they would arrange more meetings.

She walked across the bridge back to her little room and decided that, however much money and however many future plans she had, she would definitely not buy a television: she needed to think, to use all her time for thinking.

From Maria's diary that night (with a note in the margin saying: 'Not sure'):

I have discovered the reason why a man pays for a woman: he wants to be happy.

He wouldn't pay a thousand francs just to have an orgasm. He wants to be happy. I do too, everyone does, and yet no one is. What have I got to lose if, for a while, I decide to become a ... it's a difficult word to think or even write ... but let's be blunt ... what have I got to lose if I decide to become a prostitute for a while?

Honour. Dignity. Self-respect. Although, when I think about it, I've never had any of those things. I didn't ask to be born, I've never found anyone to love me, I've always made the wrong decisions – now I'm letting life decide for me.

The agency phoned the next day and asked about the photos and when the fashion show was being held, since they got a percentage of every job. Maria, realising that they knew nothing about what had happened, told them that the Arab gentleman would be in touch with them.

She went to the library and asked for some books about sex. If she was seriously considering the possibility of working – just for a year, she had told herself – in an area about which she knew nothing, the first thing she needed to know was how to behave, how to give pleasure and receive money in return.

She was most disappointed when the librarian told her that, since the library was a government-funded institution, they only had a few technical works. Maria read the index of one of these books and immediately returned it: they said nothing about happiness, they talked only about dull things such as erection, penetration, impotence, precautions ... She did for a moment consider borrowing *The Psychology of Frigidity in Women*, since, in her own case, although she very much enjoyed being possessed and penetrated by a man, she only ever reached orgasm through masturbation.

She wasn't there in search of pleasure, however, but work. She thanked the librarian, and went to a shop where she made her first investment in that possible career looming on the horizon – clothes which she considered to be sexy enough to arouse men's desire. Then she went straight to the place she had found on the map. Rue de Berne. At the top of the street was a church (oddly enough, very near the Japanese restaurant where she had had supper the night before), then some shops selling cheap watches and clocks, and, at the far end, were the clubs she had heard about, all of them closed at that hour of the day. She went for another walk around the lake, then – without a tremor of embarrassment – bought five pornographic magazines in order to study the kind of thing she would have to do, waited for darkness to fall and then went back to Rue de Berne. There she chose at random a bar with the alluringly Brazilian name of 'Copacabana'.

She hadn't decided anything, she told herself. It was just an experiment. She hadn't felt so well or so free in all the time she had been in Switzerland.

'I'm looking for work,' she told the owner, who was washing glasses behind the bar. The place consisted of a series of tables, a few sofas around the walls and, in one corner, a kind of dance floor. 'Nothing doing. If you want to work here legally you have to have a work permit.'

Maria showed him hers and the man's mood seemed to improve.

'Got any experience?'

She didn't know what to say: if she said yes, he would ask her where she had worked before. If she said no, he might turn her down.

'I'm writing a book.'

The idea had come out of nowhere, as if an invisible voice had come to her aid. She saw that the man knew she was lying, but was pretending to believe her.

'Before you make any decision, talk to some of the other girls. We get at least six Brazilian women in every night, that way you can find out exactly what to expect.'

Maria was about to say that she didn't need any advice from anyone and that, besides, she hadn't come to a decision just yet, but the man had already moved off to the other side of the bar, leaving her on her own, without even a glass of water to drink.

The women started to arrive, and the owner called over some of the Brazilians and asked them to talk to the new arrival. None of them seemed very willing; fear of competition, Maria assumed. The sound system was turned on and a few Brazilian songs were played (well, the place *was* called 'Copacabana'); then some Asiatic-looking women came in, along with others who seemed to have come straight from the snowy, romantic mountains around Geneva. She had been standing there for nearly two hours, with nothing to drink and just a few cigarettes, filled by a growing sense that she was definitely making the wrong decision – the words 'what am I doing here?' kept repeating over and over in her head – and feeling increasingly irritated by the complete lack of interest on the part of both the owner and the other women, when, finally, one of the Brazilian girls came over to her.

'What made you choose this place?'

Maria could have resorted to that story about writing a book, or she could, as she had with the Kurds, with Miró and with Fellini, simply tell the truth.

'To be perfectly honest, I don't know where to start or if I want to start.'

The other woman seemed surprised by such a frank, direct answer. She took a sip of what looked like whisky, listened to the Brazilian song they were playing, made some comment about missing her home, then said that there wouldn't be many customers that night because a big international conference being held near Geneva had been cancelled. In the end, when she saw that Maria still hadn't left, she said:

'Look, it's very simple, you just have to stick to three basic rules. First: never fall in love with anyone you work with or have sex with. Second: don't believe any promises and always get paid up front. Third: don't use drugs.'

There was a pause.

'And start now. If you go home tonight without having got your first client, you'll have second thoughts about it and you won't have the courage to come back.'

Maria had gone there more for a consultation, to get some feedback on her chances of finding a temporary job. She found herself confronted by the feeling that so often pushes people into making hasty decisions – despair.

'All right. I'll start tonight.'

She didn't mention that she had, in fact, started yesterday. The woman went up to the owner, whom she called Milan, and he came over to talk to Maria.

'Have you got nice underwear on?'

No one – her boyfriends, the Arab, her girlfriends, far less a stranger – had ever asked her that question. But that was what life was like in that place: straight to the point.

'I'm wearing pale blue pants. And no bra,' she added provocatively. But all she got was a reprimand.

'Tomorrow, wear black pants, bra and stockings. Taking off your clothes is all part of the ritual.'

Without more ado, and on the assumption now that he was talking to someone who was about to start work, Milan introduced her to the rest of the ritual: the Copacabana should be a pleasant place to spend time, not a brothel. The men came into that bar wanting to believe that they would find a lady on her own. If anyone came over to her table and wasn't intercepted en route (because some clients were 'exclusive to certain girls'), he would probably say:

'Would you like a drink?'

To which Maria could say yes or no. She was free to choose the company she kept, although it wasn't advisable to say 'no' more than once a night. If she answered in the affirmative, she should ask for a fruit juice cocktail, which just happened to be the most expensive drink on the drinks list. Absolutely no alcohol or letting the customer choose for her.

Then, she should accept any invitation to dance. Most of the clientele were familiar faces and, apart from the 'special clients', about whom he did not go into any further detail, none of them represented any danger. The police and the Department of Health demanded monthly blood samples, to check that they weren't carrying any sexually transmitted diseases. The use of condoms was obligatory, although there was no way of checking if this rule was or wasn't being followed. She should never, on any account, cause any kind of scandal – Milan was a respectable married man, concerned for his reputation and the good name of his club.

He continued explaining the ritual: after dancing, they would return to the table, and the customer, as if he were saying something highly original, would invite her to go back to his hotel with him. The normal price was three hundred and fifty francs, of which fifty francs went to Milan, for the hire of the table (a trick to avoid any future legal complications and accusations of exploiting sex for financial gain).

Maria tried to say:

'But I earned a thousand francs for ...'

The owner made as if to move off, but the other Brazilian woman, who was listening in to the conversation, said:

'She's just joking.'

And turning to Maria, she said in clear, loud Portuguese:

'This is the most expensive place in Geneva. Never do that again. He knows what the going rate is and he knows that no one pays a thousand francs to go to bed with anyone, except, of course, the "special clients", but only if you get lucky and you have the right qualifications.'

Milan's eyes – later, Maria found out that he was a Yugoslav who had been living there for twenty years – left no room for doubt.

'The price is three hundred and fifty francs.'

'Right,' said a humbled Maria.

First, he had asked about the colour of her underwear, now he was deciding how much her body was worth.

But she had no time to think, the man was still issuing instructions: she must never accept invitations to anyone's house or to a hotel that had less than five stars. If the client had nowhere to take her, she was to go to a hotel located five blocks from there, and should always take a taxi so that the women who worked in the other clubs in Rue de Berne didn't get to know her face. Maria didn't believe this last reason;

she thought that the real reason was that she might get an offer of better working conditions in another club. She kept her thoughts to herself, however; arguing about the price was bad enough.

'I'll say this again: just like policemen in the movies, never drink while on duty. I'll leave you now, it'll start getting busy soon.'

'Say thank you,' said the other Brazilian woman in Portuguese.

Maria thanked him. The man smiled, but he had not yet finished his list of recommendations:

'I forgot something: the time between ordering a drink and leaving the club should never, under any circumstances, exceed forty-five minutes – and in Switzerland, with clocks all over the place, even Yugoslavs and Brazilians must learn to be punctual. Just remember, I'm feeding my children on your commission.'

She would remember.

He gave her a glass of sparkling mineral water with a slice of lemon in it – a drink that could easily pass for a gin and tonic – and asked her to wait. Gradually the club began to fill up; men came in, looked around, sat down on their own, and immediately one of the women would go over to them, as if they were at a party where everyone has known each other for ages and as if they were just taking time out to have a little fun after a hard day at work. Every time a man found a partner, Maria gave a sigh of relief, even though she was now feeling much more comfortable. Perhaps it was because it was Switzerland, perhaps it was because, sooner or later, she would find adventure, money or a husband, as she had always dreamed she would. Perhaps – she suddenly realised – it was because it was the first time in many weeks that she had been out at night and to a place where there was music playing and where she could, now and then, hear someone speaking Portuguese. She was having fun with the other girls around her, laughing, drinking fruit juice cocktails, talking brightly.

None of them had come up to her to say hello or to wish her success in her new profession, but that was perfectly normal; after all, she was a rival, a competitor, competing for the same trophy. Instead of feeling depressed, she felt proud – she was fighting for herself, she wasn't some helpless person. She could, if she wanted to, open the door and leave that place for good, but she would always know that she had at least had the courage to come that far, to negotiate and discuss things about which she had never in her life even dared to think. She wasn't a victim of fate, she kept telling herself: she was running her own risks, pushing beyond her own limits, experiencing things which, one day, in the silence of her heart, in the tedium of old age, she would remember almost with nostalgia – however absurd that might seem.

She was sure that no one would approach her, and tomorrow it would all seem like some mad dream that she would never dare to repeat, for she had just realised that being paid a thousand francs for one night only happens once; perhaps she would be better off buying a plane ticket back to Brazil. To make the time pass more quickly, she began to work out how much each of the other girls would earn: if they went out three times a night, they would earn, for every four hours

72

of work, the equivalent of what it would have taken her two months to earn at the shop.

Was that a lot? She had earned a thousand francs for one night, but perhaps that had just been beginner's luck. At any rate, an ordinary prostitute could earn more, much more than she would ever earn teaching French back home. And all they had to do was spend some time in a bar, dance, spread their legs and that was that. They didn't even have to talk.

Money was one motivation, she thought, but was that all? Or did the people there, the customers and the women, also enjoy themselves in some way? Was the world so very different from what she had been taught in school? If you used a condom, there was no risk. Nor was there any risk of being recognised by anyone; the only people who visit Geneva – she had been told once in her French class – were people who liked going to banks. The majority of Brazilians, however, enjoy shopping, preferably in Miami or in Paris.

Three hundred Swiss francs a day, five days a week. A fortune! Why did those women keep working there when they could earn enough in a month to go back home and buy a new house for their mother? Or had they only been working there a short time?

Or – and Maria felt afraid of her own question – did they enjoy it?

Again she wished she could have a proper drink – the champagne had helped a lot the previous night.

'Would you like a drink?'

Before her stood a man in his thirties, wearing the uniform of some airline.

The world went into slow motion, and Maria had a sense of stepping out of her own body and observing herself from the outside. Deeply embarrassed, but struggling to control her blushes, she nodded and smiled, knowing that from that moment on her life had changed forever.

A fruit juice cocktail, a bit of talk, what are you doing here, it's cold, isn't it? I like this music, oh, I prefer Abba myself, the Swiss are a chilly lot, are you from Brazil? Tell me about your country. Well, there's Carnival. You Brazilian women are really pretty, you know.

Smile and accept the compliment, perhaps with a slightly shy look. Back to the dance floor, but all the time keeping an eye on Milan, who sometimes scratches his head and taps his wristwatch. The smell of the man's cologne; she realises quickly that she will have to get used to all kinds of smells. At least this is perfume. They dance very close. Another fruit juice cocktail, time is passing, didn't Milan say forty-five minutes maximum? She looks at her watch, he asks if she's expecting someone, she says a few friends of hers will be arriving in about an hour, he invites her back to his hotel. Hotel room, three hundred and fifty francs, a shower after sex (intrigued, the man remarked that no one had ever done that before). It's not Maria, it's some other person who's inside her body, who feels nothing, who mechanically goes through the motions of a ritual. She's an actress. Milan has taught her everything, even how to say goodbye to the client, she thanks him, he too feels awkward and sleepy.

She doesn't want to go back to the club, she wants to go home, but she has to go back to hand over the fifty francs, and then there's another man, another cocktail, more questions about Brazil, a hotel, another shower (this time, no comment), back to the bar where the owner takes his commission and tells her she can go, there aren't many customers tonight. She doesn't get a taxi, she walks the length of Rue de Berne, looking at the other clubs, at the shop windows full of clocks and watches, at the church on the corner (closed, always closed ...) As usual, no one looks at her.

She walks through the cold. She isn't aware of the freezing temperatures, she doesn't cry, she doesn't think about the money she has earned, she is in a kind of trance. Some people were born to face life alone, and this is neither good nor bad, it is simply life. Maria is one of those people.

She begins to try and think about what has happened: she only started work today and yet she already considers herself a professional; it's as if she started ages ago, as if she had done this all her life. She experiences a strange sense of pride; she is glad she didn't run away. Now she just has to decide whether or not to carry on. If she does carry on, then she will make sure she is the best, something she has never been before.

But life was teaching her – very fast – that only the strong survive. To be strong, she must be the best, there's no alternative.

From Maria's diary a week later:

I'm not a body with a soul, I'm a soul that has a visible part called the body. All this week, contrary to what one might expect, I have been more conscious of the presence of this soul than usual. It didn't say anything to me, didn't criticise me or feel sorry for me: it merely watched me.

Today, I realised why this was happening: it's been such a long time since I thought about love or anything called love. It seems to be running away from me, as if it wasn't important any more and didn't feel welcome. But if I don't think about love, I will be nothing.

When I went back to the Copacabana the second night, I was treated with much more respect – apparently, a lot of girls do it for one night, but can't bear to go on. Anyone who does, becomes a kind of ally, a colleague, because she can understand the difficulties and the reasons or, rather, the absence of reasons for having chosen this kind of life.

They all dream of someone who will come along and see in them a real woman – companion, lover, friend. But they all know, from the very first moment of each new encounter, that this simply isn't going to happen.

I need to write about love. I need to think and think and write and write about love – otherwise, my soul won't survive.

However important Maria thought love was, she did not forget the advice she was given on her first night and did her best to confine love to the pages of her diary. Apart from that, she tried desperately to be the best, to earn a lot of money in as short a time as possible, to think very little and to find a good reason for doing what she was doing.

That was the most difficult part: what was the real reason?

She was doing it because she needed to. This wasn't quite true – everyone needs to earn money, but not everyone chooses to live on the margins of society. She was doing it because she wanted to experience something new. No, that wasn't true either; the world was full of new experiences – like skiing or going sailing on Lake Geneva, for example – but she had never been interested. She was doing it because she had nothing to lose, because her life was one of constant, day-to-day frustration.

No, none of these answers was true, so it was best to forget all about it and simply deal with whatever lay along her particular path. She had a lot in common with the other prostitutes, and with all the other women she had known in her life, whose greatest dream was to get married and have a secure life. Those who didn't think like this either had a husband (almost a third of her colleagues were married) or were recently divorced. Because of that, and in order to understand herself, she tried – as tactfully as possible – to understand why her colleagues had chosen this profession.

She heard nothing new, but she made a list of their responses. They said they had to help out their husband (wasn't he jealous? What if one of her husband's friends came to the club one night? But Maria didn't dare to ask these questions), that they wanted to buy a house for their mother (her own excuse, apparently so noble, and the most common one), to earn enough money for their fare home (Colombians, Thais, Peruvians, Brazilians all loved this reason, even though they had earned enough money several times over and had immediately spent it, afraid to realise their dream), to have fun (this didn't really tally with the atmosphere in the club, and always rang false), they couldn't find any other kind of work (this wasn't a good reason either, Switzerland was full of jobs for cleaners, drivers and cooks).

None of them came up with any valid reason, and so she stopped trying to explain her particular Universe.

She saw that the owner, Milan, was quite right: no one ever again offered her a thousand Swiss francs for the privilege of spending a few hours with her. On the other hand, no one ever complained when she asked for three hundred and fifty francs, as if they already knew or only asked in order to humiliate her, or wanted to avoid any unpleasant surprises.

One of the girls said:

'Prostitution isn't like other businesses: beginners earn more and the more experienced earn less. Always pretend you're a beginner.'

Maria still didn't know who the 'special clients' were; they had only been mentioned on the first night and no one ever spoke of them. Gradually, she picked up the most important tricks of the trade, like never asking personal questions, smiling a lot and talking as little as possible, never arranging to meet anyone outside the club. The most important piece of advice, however, came from a Filipino woman called Nyah:

'When your client comes, you must always groan as if you were having an orgasm too. That guarantees customer loyalty.'

'But why? They're just paying for their own satisfaction.'

'No, that's where you're wrong. A man doesn't prove he's a man by getting an erection. He's only a real man if he can pleasure a woman. And if he can pleasure a prostitute, he'll think he's the best lover on the block.'

And so six months passed: Maria learned all the necessary lessons, for example, how the Copacabana worked. Since it was one of the most expensive places in Rue de Berne, the clientele was largely made up of executives, who had permission to get home late because they were out 'having supper with clients', but these 'suppers' could never last longer than eleven o'clock at night. Most of the prostitutes who worked there were aged between eighteen and twenty-two and they stayed, on average, for two years, when they would be replaced by newer recruits. They then moved to the Néon, then to the Xenium, and the price went down as the woman's age went up, and the hours of work grew fewer and fewer. They almost all ended up in the Tropical Extasy, who accepted women over thirty; but once they were there, they could only just earn enough to pay for their lunch and their rent by going with one or two students a day (the average fee per client was just about enough to buy a bottle of cheap wine).

She went to bed with many men. She didn't care how old they were or how they were dressed, but whether she said yes or no depended on how they smelled. She had nothing against cigarettes, but she hated cheap aftershave or those who didn't wash or whose clothes stank of booze. The Copacabana was a quiet place, and Switzerland was possibly the best country in the world in which to work as a prostitute, as long as you had a residence permit and a work permit, kept all your papers in order and paid your social security; Milan was always saying that he didn't want his children to see his name in the tabloid newspapers, and so he was as strict as a policeman when it came to keeping an eye on his 'employees'.

Once you had got past the barrier of the first or second night, it was a profession much like any other, in which you worked hard, fought off the competition, tried to maintain standards, put in the necessary hours, got a bit stressed out, complained about your workload, and rested on Sundays. Most of the prostitutes had some kind of religious faith, and attended their respective churches and masses, said their prayers and had their encounters with God.

Maria, however, was struggling in the pages of her diary not to lose her soul. She discovered, to her surprise, that one in every five clients didn't want her in order to have sex, but simply to talk a little. They paid for the bar tab and the hotel room, and when the moment came for them both to take off their clothes, the man would say, no, that won't be necessary. They wanted to talk about the pressures of work, about their unfaithful wife, about how lonely they felt, how they had no one to talk to (something she knew about all too well).

At first, she found this very odd. Then, one night, she went to the hotel with an arrogant Frenchman, a headhunter for top executive jobs (he told her this as if he were telling her the most fascinating thing in the world), and this is what he said:

'Do you know who the loneliest person in the world is? The executive with a successful career, earning an enormous salary, trusted by those above and below him, with a family to go on holiday with and children who he helps out with their homework, but who is then approached by someone like me and asked the following question: "How would you like to change your job and earn twice as much?"

'The executive, who has every reason to feel wanted and happy, becomes the most miserable creature on the planet. Why? Because he has no one to talk to. He is tempted to accept my offer, but he can't talk about it to his work colleagues because they would do everything they could to persuade him to stay. He can't talk about it to his wife, who has been his companion in his rise up the ladder of success and understands a great deal about security, but nothing about taking risks. He can't talk to anyone about it and there he is confronted by the biggest decision of his life. Can you imagine how that man feels?'

No, that man wasn't the loneliest person in the world. Maria knew the loneliest person on the face of this Earth: herself. Nevertheless, she agreed with her client, hoping to get a big tip, which she did. But his words made her realise that she needed to find some way of freeing her clients from the enormous pressure they all seemed to be under; this meant both improving the quality of her services and the chance of earning some extra money.

When she realised that releasing tension in the soul could be as lucrative as releasing tension in the body, if not more lucrative, she started going to the library again. She began asking for books about marital problems, psychology and politics; the librarian was delighted to see that the young woman of whom she had grown so fond had stopped think-ing about sex and was now concentrating on more important matters. Maria became a regular reader of newspapers, especially, where possible, the financial pages, because the majority of her clients were business executives. She sought out self-help books, because her clients nearly all asked for her advice. She read studies of the human emotions, because all her clients were in some kind of emotional pain. Maria was a respectable, rather unusual prostitute, and after six months, she had acquired a large, faithful, very select clientele, thus arousing the envy and jealousy, but also the admiration, of her colleagues.

As for sex, it had as yet added nothing to her life: it was just a matter of opening her legs, asking them to use a condom, moaning a bit in the hope of getting a better tip (thanks to the Filipino woman, Nyah, she had learned that moaning could earn her another fifty francs), and taking a shower afterwards, hoping that the water would wash her soul clean. Nothing out of the ordinary and no kissing. For a prostitute, the kiss was sacred. Nyah had taught her to keep her kisses for the love of her life, just like in the story of Sleeping Beauty; a kiss that would waken her from her slumbers and return her to the world of fairy tales, in which Switzerland was once more the country of chocolate, cows and clocks.

And no orgasms either, no pleasure or excitement. In her search to be the very best, Maria had watched a few porn movies, hoping to pick up tips for her work. She had seen a lot of interesting things, but had preferred not to try any of them out on her clients because they took too long, and Milan was happiest when the women averaged three men a night.

By the end of the six months, Maria had sixty thousand Swiss francs in a bank account; she ate in better restaurants, had bought a TV (she never watched it, but she liked to have it there) and was now seriously considering moving to a better apartment. Although she could easily afford to buy books, she continued going to the library, which was her bridge to the real world, a more solid and enduring world. She enjoyed chatting to the librarian, who was happy because Maria had perhaps found a boyfriend and a job, although she never asked, the Swiss being naturally shy and discreet (a complete fallacy, because in the Copacabana and in bed, they were as uninhibited, joyful or neurotic as any other nationality).

From Maria's diary, one warm Sunday evening:

All men, tall or short, arrogant or unassuming, friendly or cold, have one characteristic in common: when they come to the club, they are afraid. The more experienced amongst them hide their fear by talking loudly, the more inhibited cannot hide their feelings and start drinking to see if they can drive the fear away. But I am convinced that, with a few very rare exceptions – the 'special clients' to whom Milan has not yet introduced me – they are all afraid.

Afraid of what? I'm the one who should be shaking. I'm the one who leaves the club and goes off to a strange hotel, and I'm not the one with the superior physical strength or the weapons. Men are very strange, and I don't just mean the ones who come to the Copacabana, but all the men I've ever met. They can beat you up, shout at you, threaten you, and yet they're scared to death of women really. Perhaps not the woman they married, but there's always one woman who frightens them and forces them to submit to her caprices. Even if it's their own mother.

The men she had met since she arrived in Geneva always did everything they could to appear confident, as if they were in perfect control of the world and of their own lives; Maria, however, could see in their eyes that they were afraid of their wife, the feeling of panic that they might not be able to get an erection, that they might not seem manly enough even to the ordinary prostitute whom they were paying for her services. If they went to a shop and didn't like the shoes they had bought, they would be quite prepared to go back, receipt in hand, and demand a refund. And yet, even though they were paying for some female company, if they didn't manage to get an erection, they would be too ashamed ever to go back to the same club again because they would assume that all the other women there would know.

'I'm the one who should feel ashamed for being unable to arouse them, but, no, they always blame themselves.'

To avoid such embarrassments, Maria always tried to put men at their ease, and if someone seemed drunker or more fragile than usual, she would avoid full sex and concentrate instead on caresses and masturbation, which always seemed to please them immensely, absurd though this might seem, since they could perfectly well masturbate on their own.

She had to make sure that they didn't feel ashamed. These men, so powerful and arrogant at work, constantly having to deal with employees, customers, suppliers, prejudices, secrets, posturings, hypocrisy, fear and oppression, ended

87

their day in a nightclub and they didn't mind spending three hundred and fifty Swiss francs to stop being themselves for a night.

'For a night? Now come on, Maria, you're exaggerating. It's really only forty-five minutes, and if you allow time for taking off clothes, making some phoney gesture of affection, having a bit of banal conversation and getting dressed again, the amount of time spent actually having sex is about eleven minutes.'

Eleven minutes. The world revolved around something that only took eleven minutes.

And because of those eleven minutes in any one twenty-four-hour day (assuming that they all made love to their wives every day, which is patently absurd and a complete lie) they got married, supported a family, put up with screaming kids, thought up ridiculous excuses to justify getting home late, ogled dozens, if not hundreds of other women with whom they would like to go for a walk around Lake Geneva, bought expensive clothes for themselves and even more expensive clothes for their wives, paid prostitutes to try to give them what they were missing, and thus sustained a vast industry of cosmetics, diet foods, exercise, pornography and power, and yet when they got together with other men, contrary to popular belief, they never talked about women. They talked about jobs, money and sport.

Something was very wrong with civilisation, and it wasn't the destruction of the Amazon rainforest or the ozone layer, the death of the panda, cigarettes, carcinogenic foodstuffs or prison conditions, as the newspapers would have it.

It was precisely the thing she was working with: sex.

But Maria wasn't there to save humanity, but to increase her bank balance, survive another six months of solitude and another six months of the choice she had made, send a regular monthly sum of money to her mother (who was thrilled to learn that the earlier absence of money had been due to the Swiss post, so much less efficient than the Brazilian postal system), and to buy all the things she had always dreamed of and never had. She moved to a much better apartment, with central heating (although the summer had already arrived), and from her window she could see a church, a Japanese restaurant, a supermarket and a very nice café, where she used to sit and read the newspapers. Otherwise, just as she had promised herself, it was a question of putting up with the same old routine: go to the Copacabana, have a drink and a dance, what do you think of Brazil, then back to his hotel, get the money up front, have a little conversation and know precisely which points to touch – on both body and soul, but mainly the soul – give some advice on personal problems, be his friend for half an hour, of which eleven minutes would be spent in opening her legs, closing her legs and pretending to moan with pleasure. Thanks very much, see you next week, you're very manly, you know, tell me how things went next time we meet, oh, that's very generous of you, but really there's no need, it's been a pleasure to spend time with you.

And, above all, never fall in love. That was the most important and most sensible piece of advice that the other Brazilian woman had given her, before she disappeared, perhaps because she herself had fallen in love. Because, incredible though it may seem, in just two months of working there, Maria had had several proposals of marriage, of which at least three were serious: the director of a firm of accountants, the pilot she went with on the very first night, and the owner of a shop specialising in knives. All three had promised 'to take her away from that life' and to give her a nice house, a future, perhaps children and grandchildren.

And all for eleven minutes a day? It wasn't possible. After her experiences at the Copacabana, she knew that she wasn't the only person who felt lonely. Human beings can withstand a week without water, two weeks without food, many years of homelessness, but not loneliness. It is the worst of all tortures, the worst of all sufferings. Like her, these men, and the many others who sought her company, were all tormented by that same destructive feeling, the sense that no one else on the planet cared about them.

In order to avoid being tempted by love, she kept her heart for her diary. She entered the Copacabana with only her body and her brain, which was growing sharper and more perceptive all the time. She had managed to persuade herself that there was some important reason why she had come to Geneva and ended up in Rue de Berne, and every time she borrowed a book from the library she was confirmed in her view that no one wrote properly about the eleven most important minutes of the day. Perhaps that was her destiny, however hard it might seem at the moment: to write a book, relating her story, her adventure.

That was it, her adventure. Although it was a forbidden word that no one dared to speak, and which most people preferred to watch on the television, in films that were shown over and over at all times of the day and night, that was what she was looking for. It was a word that evoked deserts, journeys to unknown places, idle conversations with mysterious men on a boat in the middle of a river, plane journeys, cinema studios, tribes of Indians, glaciers and Africa.

She liked the idea of a book and had even thought of a title: Eleven Minutes.

She began to put clients into three categories: the Exterminators (in homage to a film she had enjoyed hugely), who arrived stinking of drink, pretending not to look at anyone, but convinced that everyone was looking at them, dancing only briefly and then getting straight down to the business of going back to their hotel. The Pretty Woman type (again named after a film), who tried to appear elegant, gentlemanly, affectionate, as if the world depended on such kindness in order to continue turning on its axis, as if they had just been walking down the street and had come into the club by chance; they were always very sweet at first and rather uncertain when they got to the hotel, but, because of that, they always proved even more demanding than the Exterminators. And lastly, there was The Godfather type (named after yet another film), who treated a woman's body as if it were a piece of merchandise. They were the most genuine; they danced, talked, never gave tips, knew what they were buying and how much it was worth, and never let themselves be taken in by anything the woman of their choice might say. They were the only ones who, in a very subtle way, knew the meaning of the word 'Adventure'.

From Maria's diary, on a day when she had her period and couldn't work:

If I were to tell someone about my life today, I could do it in a way that would make them think me a brave, happy, independent woman. Rubbish: I am not even allowed to mention the only word that is more important than the eleven minutes – love.

All my life, I thought of love as some kind of voluntary enslavement. Well, that's a lie: freedom only exists when love is present. The person who gives him or herself wholly, the person who feels freest, is the person who loves most wholeheartedly.

And the person who loves wholeheartedly feels free.

That is why, regardless of what I might experience, do or learn, nothing makes sense. I hope this time passes quickly, so that I can resume my search for myself – in the form of a man who understands me and does not make me suffer.

But what am I saying? In love, no one can harm anyone else; we are each of us responsible for our own feelings and cannot blame someone else for what we feel.

It hurt when I lost each of the various men I fell in love with. Now, though, I am convinced that no one loses anyone, because no one owns anyone.

That is the true experience of freedom: having the most important thing in the world without owning it.

Another three months passed, and autumn came, as did the date marked on the calendar: ninety days until her return journey home. Everything had happened so quickly and so slowly, she thought, realising that time exists in two different dimensions, depending on one's state of mind, but in both sorts of time her adventure was drawing to a close. She could, of course, continue, but she could not forget the sad smile of the invisible woman who had accompanied her on that walk around the lake, telling her that things weren't that simple. However tempted she was to continue, however prepared she was for the challenges she had met on her path, all these months living alone with herself had taught her that there is always a right moment to stop something. In ninety days' time she would return to the interior of Brazil, where she would buy a small farm (she had earned rather more than she had expected), a few cows (Brazilian, not Swiss), invite her mother and father to come and live with her, take on a couple of workers, and set the business in motion.

Although she believed that love is the only true experience of freedom, and that no one can possess anyone else, she still harboured a secret desire for revenge, and this formed part of her triumphal return to Brazil. After setting up the farm, she would go back to her hometown and make a large deposit in Swiss francs at the bank where the boy who had two-timed her with her best friend was working. 'Hi, how are you? Don't you remember me?' he would say.

She would pretend to be trying hard to remember and would end up saying that, no, she didn't, she had just come back from a year in EU-ROPE (she would say this very slowly so that all his colleagues would hear). Or, rather, SWIT-ZER-LAND (that would sound more exotic and adventurous than France), where they have the best banks in the world.

Who was he? He would mention their schooldays. She would say: 'Ah, yes, I think I remember ...', but from her face it would be clear that she didn't. Vengeance would be hers, and then it would just be a matter of working hard, and when the farm was doing as well as she expected, she would be able to devote herself to the thing that mattered most in her life: finding her true love, the man who had been waiting for her all these years, but whom she had not yet had the chance to meet.

Maria decided to forget all about writing the book entitled *Eleven Minutes*. Now she needed to concentrate on the farm, on her future plans, otherwise, she would end up postponing her trip, a fatal risk.

That afternoon, she went off to meet her best – and only – friend, the librarian. She asked for a book on cattle-raising and farm administration. The librarian said:

'You know, a few months ago, when you came here looking for books about sex, I began to fear for you. So many pretty young girls let themselves be seduced by the illusion of easy money, forgetting that, one day, they'll be old and will have missed out on meeting the love of their life.'

'Do you mean prostitution?'

'That's a very strong word.'

'As I said, I'm working for a company that imports and exports meat. But if I had to become a prostitute, would the consequences be so very grave if I stopped at the right moment? After all, being young inevitably means making mistakes.'

'That's what all the drug addicts say, that you just have to know when to stop. But none of them do.'

'You must have been very pretty when you were younger and you were brought up in a country that respects its inhabitants. Was that enough for you to be happy?'

'I'm proud of how I dealt with any obstacles in my life.'

Should she go on, thought the librarian. Yes, why not, the girl needed to learn a bit about life.

'I had a happy childhood, I studied at one of the best schools in Berne, then I came to work in Geneva, where I met and married the man I loved. I did everything for him and he did everything for me; time passed and he retired. When he was free to do exactly what he wanted with his time, his eyes grew sadder, because he had probably never really thought about himself all his life. We never had any serious arguments or any great excitements, he was never unfaithful to me and was never rude to me in public. We lived a very ordinary life, so much so that, without a job to do, he felt useless, unimportant, and, a year later, he died of cancer.'

She was telling the truth, but felt that she might be having a negative influence on the girl standing before her.

'I still think it's best to lead a life without surprises,' she concluded. 'If we hadn't, my husband might have died even earlier, who knows.'

Maria left, determined to learn all about farming. Since she had the afternoon free, she decided to go for a stroll and, in the upper part of the city, came across a small yellow plaque bearing a drawing of a sun and an inscription: 'Road to Santiago'. What did it mean? There was a bar on the other side of the road, and since she had now learned to ask about anything she didn't understand, she resolved to go in and ask.

'I've no idea,' said the girl serving behind the bar. It was a very expensive place, and the coffee cost three times the normal price. Since she had money, though, and now that she was there, she ordered a coffee and decided to spend the next hour or so learning all there was to know about farm administration. She opened the book eagerly, but found it impossible to concentrate – it was *so* boring. It would be much more interesting to talk to one of her clients about it; they always knew how best to handle money. She paid for her coffee, got up, thanked the girl who had served her, left a large tip (she had invented a superstitious belief according to which the more you gave, the more you got back), went over to the door, and, without realising the importance of that moment, heard the words that would change forever her plans, her future, her farm, her idea of happiness, her female soul, her male approach to life, her place in the world.

'Hang on a moment.'

Surprised, she glanced to one side. This was a respectable bar, it wasn't the Copacabana, where men had the right to say that, although the women could always respond: 'No, I'm leaving and you can't stop me.'

She was about to ignore the remark, but her curiosity got the better of her, and she turned towards the voice. She saw a very strange scene: kneeling on the floor, with various paint-brushes scattered around him, was a long-haired young man of about thirty (or should she have said: a boy of about thirty? Her world had aged very fast), who was making a drawing of a gentleman sitting in a chair, with a glass of anisette beside him. She hadn't noticed them when she came in.

'Don't go. I've nearly finished this portrait, and I'd like to paint you as well.'

Maria replied – and as she did so, she created the link that was lacking in the universe.

'No, I'm not interested.'

'You've got a special light about you. Let me at least do a sketch.'

What was a 'sketch'? What did he mean by 'a special light'? Besides, she was vain enough to want to have her portrait painted by someone who appeared to be a serious artist. Her imagination took flight. What if he was really famous? She would be immortalised forever in a painting that would be exhibited in Paris or in Salvador da Bahia! She would become a legend!

On the other hand, what was the man doing, surrounded by all that clutter, in an expensive, perhaps usually crowded café?

Guessing her thoughts, the waitress said softly:

'He's a very well-known artist.'

Her intuition had been right. Maria tried not to show her feelings and to remain calm.

'He comes here now and again, and he always brings an important client with him. He says he likes the atmosphere, that it inspires him; he's doing a painting of people who represent the city. It was commissioned by the town hall.'

Maria looked at the subject of the portrait. Again the waitress read her thoughts.

'He's a chemist who apparently made some really revolutionary discovery. He won the Nobel Prize.'

'Don't go,' said the painter again. 'I'll be finished in five minutes. Order what you like and put it on my bill.'

As if hypnotised, she sat down at the bar, ordered an anisette (she wasn't used to drinking, and the only thing that occurred to her was to order the same as the Nobel prizewinner), and watched the man working. 'I don't represent the city, so he must be interested in something else. But he's not really my type,' she thought automatically, repeating what she always said to herself, ever since she had been working at the Copacabana; it was her salvation, her voluntary denial of the traps set by the heart. Having cleared that up, she didn't mind waiting a while – perhaps the waitress was right, perhaps this man could open doors to a world of which she knew nothing.

She watched how quickly and adroitly he put the finishing touches to his work; it was apparently a very large canvas, but it was all rolled up, and so she couldn't see what other faces he had painted. What if this was a new opportunity? The man (she had decided that he was a 'man' and not a 'boy', because otherwise she would start to feel old before her time) didn't seem the sort likely to make that kind of proposal just in order to spend the night with her. Five minutes later, as promised, he had finished his work, while Maria concentrated hard on thinking about Brazil, about her brilliant future there, and her complete lack of interest in meeting new people who might jeopardise all her plans.

'Thanks, you can move now,' said the painter to the chemist, who seemed to awaken from a dream.

And turning to Maria, he said simply:

'Sit in that corner and make yourself comfortable. The light is wonderful.'

As if everything had been ordained by fate, as if it were the most natural thing in the world, as if she had known this man all her life or had already lived this moment in dreams and now knew what to do in reality, Maria picked up her glass of anisette, her bag, and the books on farm management, and went over to the place indicated by the man – a table near the window. He brought his brushes, the large canvas, a series of small glass bottles full of various colours and a packet of cigarettes, and knelt at her feet.

'Now don't move.'

'That's asking a lot; my life is in constant motion.'

Maria thought she was being terribly witty, but the man ignored her remark. Trying to appear natural, because she found the way the man looked at her most discomfiting, she pointed across the road at the plaque:

'What is the "Road to Santiago"?'

'It's a pilgrimage route. In the Middle Ages, people from all over Europe would come along this street, heading for a city in Spain, Santiago de Compostela.'

He folded over one part of the canvas and prepared his brushes. Maria still didn't know quite what to do.

'Do you mean that if I followed that street, I'd eventually get to Spain?'

'Yes, in two or three months' time. But can I just ask you a favour? Stop talking; it will only take about ten minutes. And take that package off the table.'

'They're books,' she said, slightly irritated by his authoritarian tone. She wanted him to know that he was kneeling before a cultivated woman, who spent her time in libraries not shops. But he himself picked up the package and placed it unceremoniously on the floor.

She had failed to impress him. Not, of course, that she was remotely interested in impressing him; she was off-duty now and would save her seductive powers for later, for men who would pay handsomely for her efforts. Why bother striking up a relationship with a painter who might not even have enough money to buy her a coffee? A man of thirty shouldn't wear his hair so long, it looked ridiculous. Why did she assume he had no money? The waitress had said he was wellknown, or was it just the chemist who was famous? She studied his clothes, but that didn't help; life had taught her that the men who took least care of their appearance – as with this painter – always seemed to have more money than the men in suits and ties.

'What am I doing thinking about this man? What interests me is the painting.'

Ten minutes of her time was not such a high price to pay for the chance of being immortalised in a painting. She saw that he was painting her alongside the prizewinning chemist and she began to wonder if, after all, he would want some kind of payment.

'Turn towards the window.'

Again she obeyed unquestioningly, which was not at all like her. She sat looking at the people passing by, at the plaque with the name of that road on it, thinking about how that road had been there for centuries, how it had survived progress and all the changes that had taken place in the world and in mankind. Perhaps it was a good omen, perhaps that painting would share the same fate and still be on display in a museum in the city in five hundred years' time ...

The man started drawing, and, as the work progressed, she lost that initial sense of excitement and, instead, began to feel utterly insignificant. When she had gone into the café, she had been a very confident woman, capable of making an extremely difficult decision – leaving a job that earned her lots of money – and taking up a still more difficult challenge – running a farm back in her own country. Now, all her feelings of insecurity about the world seemed to have resurfaced, a luxury no prostitute can allow herself.

She finally worked out why she was feeling so uncomfortable: for the first time in many months, someone was looking at her not as an object, not even as a woman, but as something she could not even comprehend; the closest she could come to putting it into words was: 'he's seeing my soul, my fears, my fragility, my inability to deal with a world which I pretend to master, but about which I know nothing'.

Ridiculous, pure fantasy.

'I'd like ...'

'Please, don't talk,' said the man. 'I can see your light now.'

No one had ever said anything like that to her before. 'I can see your firm breasts', 'I can see your nicely rounded thighs', 'I can see in you the exotic beauty of the tropics', or, at most, 'I can see that you want to leave this life – let me set you up in an apartment'. She was used to comments like that, but her light? Did he mean the evening light?

'Your personal light,' he said, realising that she didn't know what he was talking about.

Her personal light. Well, how wrong could he be, that innocent painter, who obviously hadn't learned much about life in his thirty-odd years. But then, as everyone knows, women mature more quickly than men, and although Maria might not spend sleepless nights pondering her particular philosophical problems, she knew one thing: she did not have what that painter called 'light' and which she took to mean 'a special glow'. She was just like everyone else, she endured her loneliness in silence, tried to justify everything she did, pretended to be strong when she was feeling weak or weak when she was feeling strong, she had renounced love and taken up a dangerous profession, but now, as that work was coming to an end, she had plans for the future and regrets about the past, and someone like that doesn't have a 'special glow'. That must just be his way of keeping her quiet and still and happy to be there, playing the fool.

Personal light, indeed. He could have said something else, like 'you've got a lovely profile'.

How does light enter a house? Through the open windows. How does light enter a person? Through the open door of love. And her door was definitely shut. He must be a terrible painter; he didn't understand anything.

'I've finished,' he said and started collecting up his things.

Maria didn't move. She felt like asking if she could see the painting, but that might seem rude, as if she didn't trust what he had done. Curiosity, however, got the better of her; she asked and he concurred. He had painted only her face; it looked like her, but if, one day, she had seen that painting, not knowing who the model was, she would have said that it was someone much stronger, someone full of a 'light' she didn't see reflected in the mirror.

'My name's Ralf Hart. If you like, I can buy you another drink.'

'No, thank you.'

It would seem that the encounter was now taking a sadly foreseeable turn: man tries to seduce woman.

'Two more anisettes, please,' he said, ignoring Maria's answer.

What else did she have to do? Read a boring book about farm management. Walk around the lake, as she had hundreds of times before. Or talk to someone who had seen in her a light of which she knew nothing, and on the very date marked on the calendar as the beginning of the end of her 'experience'.

'What do you do?'

That was the question she did not want to hear, the question that had made her avoid other encounters when, for one reason or another, someone had approached her (though given the natural discretion of the Swiss, this happened only rarely). What possible answer could she give?

'I work in a nightclub.'

Right. An enormous load fell from her shoulders, and she was pleased with all that she had learned since she had arrived in Switzerland; ask questions (Who are the Kurds? What is the road to Santiago?) and answer (I work in a night-club) without worrying about what other people might think.

'I have a feeling I've seen you before.'

Maria sensed that he wanted to take things further, and she savoured her small victory; the painter who, minutes before, had been giving orders and had seemed so utterly sure of what he wanted, had now gone back to being a man like any other man, full of insecurity when confronted by a woman he didn't know.

'And what are those books?'

She showed them to him. Farm administration. The man seemed to grow even more insecure.

'Are you a sex worker?'

He had shown his cards. Was she dressed like a prosti-tute? Anyway, she needed to gain time. She was watching herself; this was beginning to prove an interesting game, and she had absolutely nothing to lose.

'Is that all men think about?'

He put the books back in the bag.

'Sex and farm management. How very dull.'

What! It was suddenly her turn to feel put on the spot. How dare he speak ill of her profession? He still didn't know exactly what she did, though, he was just trying out a hunch, but she had to give him an answer.

'Well, I can't think of anything duller than painting; a static thing, a movement frozen in time, a photograph that is never faithful to the original. A dead thing that is no longer of any interest to anyone, apart from painters, who are people who think they're important and cultivated, but who haven't evolved with the rest of the world. Have you ever heard of Joan Miró? Well, I hadn't until an Arab in a restaurant mentioned the name, but knowing the name didn't change anything in my life.'

She wondered if she had gone too far, but then the drinks arrived and the conversation was interrupted. They sat saying nothing for a while. Maria thought it was probably time to leave, and perhaps Ralf Hart thought the same. But before them stood those two glasses full of that disgusting drink, and that was a reason for them to continue sitting there together.

'Why the book on farm management?'

'What do you mean?'

'I've been to Rue de Berne. When you said you worked in a nightclub, I remembered that I'd seen you before in that very expensive place. I didn't think of it while I was painting, though: your "light" was so strong.'

Maria felt the floor beneath her feet give way. For the first time, she felt ashamed of what she did, even though she had no reason to; she was working to keep herself and her family. He was the one who should feel ashamed of going to Rue de Berne; all the possible charm of that meeting had suddenly vanished.

'Listen, Mr Hart, I may be a Brazilian, but I've lived in Switzerland for nine months now. I've learned that the reason the Swiss are so discreet is because they live in a very small country where almost everyone knows everyone else, as we have just discovered, which is why no one ever asks what other people do. Your remark was both inappropriate and very rude, but if your aim was to humiliate me in order to make yourself feel better, you're wasting your time. Thanks for the anisette, which is disgusting, by the way, but which I will drink to the last drop. I will then smoke a cigarette, and, finally, I'll get up and leave. But you can leave right now, if you want; we can't have famous painters sitting at the same table as a prostitute. Because that's what I am, you see. A prostitute. I'm a prostitute through and through, from head to toe, and I don't care who knows. That's my one great virtue: I refuse to deceive myself or you. Because it's not worth it, because you don't merit a lie. Imagine if that famous chemist over there were to find out what I am.'

She began to speak more loudly.

'Yes, I'm a prostitute! And do you know what? It's set me free – knowing that I'll be leaving this godawful place in exactly ninety days' time, with loads of money, far better educated, capable of choosing a good bottle of wine, with my handbag stuffed with photographs of the snow, and knowing all there is to know about men!'

The waitress was listening, horrified. The chemist seemed not to notice. Perhaps it was just the alcohol talking, or the feeling that soon she would once more be a woman from the interior of Brazil, or perhaps it was the sheer joy of being able to say what she did and to laugh at the shocked reactions, the critical looks, the scandalised gestures.

'Do you understand, Mr Hart? I'm a prostitute through and through, from head to toe – and that's my one great quality, my virtue!'

He said nothing. He didn't even move. Maria felt her confidence returning.

'And you, sir, are a painter with no understanding of your models. Perhaps the chemist sitting over there, dozing, lost to the world, is really a railway worker. Perhaps none of the other people in your painting are what they seem. I can't understand otherwise how you could possibly say that you could see a "special light" in a woman who, as you discovered while you were painting, IS NOTHING BUT A PROSTI-TUTE!'

These last words were spoken very slowly and loudly. The chemist woke up and the waitress brought the bill.

'This has nothing to do with you as prostitute, but with you as woman.' Ralf ignored the proffered bill and replied equally slowly, but quietly. 'You have a glow about you. The light that comes from sheer willpower, the light of someone who has made important sacrifices in the name of things she thinks are important. It's in your eyes – the light is in your eyes.'

Maria felt disarmed; he had not taken up her challenge. She had wanted to believe that he was simply trying to pick her up. She was not allowed to think – at least not for the next ninety days – that there were interesting men on the face of the Earth.

'You see that glass of anisette before you?' he went on. 'Now, you just see the anisette. I, on the other hand, because I need to be inside everything I do, see the plant it came from, the storms the plant endured, the hand that picked the grain, the voyage by ship from another land, the smells and colours with which the plant allowed itself to be imbued before it was placed in the alcohol. If I were to paint this scene, I would paint all those things, even though, when you saw the painting, you would think you were looking at a simple glass of anisette.

'In just the same way, while you were gazing out at the street and thinking – because I know you were – about the road to Santiago, I painted your childhood, your adolescence, your lost, broken dreams, your dreams for the future, and your will – which is what most intrigues me. When you saw your portrait ...'

Maria put up her guard, knowing that it would be very difficult to lower it again later on.

'... I saw that light ... even though all that was before me was a woman who looked like you.'

Again that constrained silence. Maria looked at her watch.

'I have to go in a moment. Why did you say that sex is boring?'

'You should know that better than me.'

'I know because it's my job. I do the same thing every day. But you're a young man of thirty ...'

'Twenty-nine.'

'... young, attractive, famous, who should be interested in things like that, and who shouldn't have to go to Rue de Berne looking for company.'

'Well, I did. I went to bed with a few of your colleagues, but not because I had any problem finding female company. The problem lies with me.'

Maria felt a pang of jealousy, and was terrified. She really must leave.

'It was my last try. I've given up now,' said Ralf, starting to pick up the painting materials scattered on the floor.

'Have you got some physical problem?'

'No, I'm just not interested.'

This wasn't possible.

'Pay the bill and let's go for a walk. I think a lot of people feel the same, but no one ever says so. It's good to talk to someone so honest.'

They set off along the road to Santiago, which first climbed and then descended down to the river, then to the lake, then on to the mountains, to end in some distant place in Spain. They passed people going back to work after lunch, mothers with their prams, tourists taking photographs of the splendid fountain in the middle of the lake, Muslim women in their headscarves, boys and girls out jogging, all of them pilgrims in search of that mythological city, Santiago de Compostela, which might not even exist, which might be a legend in which people need to believe in order to give meaning to their lives. Along this road walked by so many people, over so many years, went that man with long hair, carrying a heavy bag full of brushes, paints, canvas and pencils, and that woman, slightly younger, with her bag full of books about farm management. It did not occur to either of them to ask why they were making that pilgrimage together, it was the most natural thing in the world; he knew everything about her, although she knew nothing about him.

Which is why she decided to ask – now that her policy was always to ask. At first, he reacted shyly, but she knew how to wheedle information out of men, and he ended up telling her that he had been married twice (a record for a twenty-nine-year-old!), had travelled widely, met kings and queens and famous actors, been to unforgettable parties. He had been born in Geneva, but had lived in Madrid, Amsterdam, New York, and in a city in the south of France, called Tarbes, which wasn't on any of the usual tourist circuits, but which he loved because it was so close to the mountains and because its inhabitants were so warm-hearted. He had been discovered as an artist when he was only twenty, when an important art dealer happened to visit a Japanese restaurant in Geneva decorated with his work. He had earned a lot of money, he was young and healthy, he could do anything, go anywhere, meet anyone he liked, he had known all the pleasures a man could know, he did what he most enjoyed doing, and yet, despite everything, fame, money, women, travel, he was unhappy, and had only one joy in his life – his work.

'Were you very hurt by women?' she asked, realising at once what an idiotic question it was, straight out of some manual entitled *Everything Women Should Know If They Want to Get Their Man*.

'No, they never hurt me. I was very happy in both my marriages. I was unfaithful and so were they, just like any other normal couple. Then, after a while, I simply lost interest in sex. I still felt love, still needed company, but sex ... but, why are we talking about sex?'

'Because, as you yourself said, I'm a prostitute.'

'My life isn't very interesting really. I'm an artist who found success very young, which is rare, and even rarer in the world of painting. I could paint anything now and it would be worth a fortune, which, of course, infuriates the critics because they think they are the only ones who know about "art". Other people think I've got all the answers, and the less I say, the more intelligent they think I am.'

He went on talking about his life, how every week he was invited to something somewhere in the world. He had an agent who lived in Barcelona – did she know where that was? Yes, Maria knew, it was in Spain. This agent dealt with everything to do with money, invitations, exhibitions, but never pressured him to do anything he didn't want to do, now that, after years of work, there was a steady demand for his paintings.

'Do you find my story interesting?' he asked, and his voice betrayed a touch of insecurity.

'It's certainly an unusual one. Lots of people would like to be in your shoes.'

Ralf wanted to know about Maria.

'Well, there are three of me, really, depending on who I'm with. There's the Innocent Girl, who gazes admiringly at the man, pretending to be impressed by his tales of power and glory. Then there's the Femme Fatale, who pounces on the most insecure and, by doing so, takes control of the situation and relieves them of responsibility, because then they don't have to worry about anything. And, finally, there's the Understanding Mother, who looks after those in need of advice and who listens with an all-comprehending air to stories that go in one ear and out the other. Which of the three would you like to meet?'

'You.'

Maria told him everything, because she needed to – it was the first time she had done so since she left Brazil. She realised that, despite her somewhat unconventional job, nothing very exciting had happened apart from that week in Rio and her first month in Switzerland. Otherwise, it had been home, work, home, work – and nothing else.

When she finished speaking, they were sitting in another bar, this time on the other side of the city, far from the road to Santiago, each of them thinking about what fate had reserved for the other.

'Did I leave anything out?' she asked.

'How to say "goodbye".'

Yes, it had not been an afternoon like any other. She felt tense and anxious, for she had opened a door which she didn't know how to close.

'When can I see the whole painting?'

Ralf gave her the card of his agent in Barcelona.

'Phone her in about six months' time, if you're still in Europe. *The Faces of Geneva*, famous people and anonymous people. It will be exhibited for the first time in a gallery in Berlin. Then it will tour Europe.'

Maria remembered her calendar, the ninety days that remained, and the dangers posed by any relationship, any bond. She thought:

'What is more important in life? Living or pretending to live? Should I take a risk and say that this has been the loveliest afternoon I've spent in all the time I've been here? Should I thank him for listening to me without criticism and without comment? Or should I simply don the armour of the woman with willpower, with the "special light", and leave without saying anything?'

While they were walking along the road to Santiago and while she was listening to herself telling him about her life, she had been a happy woman. She could content herself with that; it was enough of a gift from life.

'I'll come and see you,' said Ralf Hart.

'No, don't. I'll be going back to Brazil soon. We have nothing more to give each other.'

'I'll come and see you as a client.'

'That would be humiliating for me.'

'I'll come and see you so that you can save me.'

He had made that comment early on, about his lack of interest in sex. She wanted to tell him that she felt the same, but she stopped herself – she had said 'no' too many times; it would be best to say nothing.

How pathetic. There she was with the little boy again, only he wasn't asking her for a pencil now, just a little company. She looked at her own past, and, for the first time, she forgave herself: it hadn't been her fault, but the fault of that insecure little boy, who had given up after the first attempt. They were children and that's how children are – neither she nor the boy had been in the wrong, and that gave her a great sense of relief, made her feel better; she hadn't betrayed the first opportunity that life had presented her with. We all do the same thing: it's part of the initiation of every human being in search of his or her other half; these things happen.

Now, though, the situation was different. However convincing her reasons (I'm going back to Brazil, I work in a nightclub, we hardly know each other, I'm not interested in sex, I don't want anything to do with love, I need to learn how to manage a farm, I don't understand painting, we live in different worlds), life had thrown down a challenge. She wasn't a child any more, she had to choose.

She preferred to say nothing. She shook his hand, as was the custom there, and went home. If he was the man she wanted him to be, he would not be intimidated by her silence.

Extract from Maria's diary, written that same day:

Today, while we were walking around the lake, along that strange road to Santiago, the man who was with me – a painter, with a life entirely different from mine – threw a pebble into the water. Small circles appeared where the pebble fell, which grew and grew until they touched a duck that happened to be passing and which had nothing to do with the pebble. Instead of being afraid of that unexpected wave, he decided to play with it.

Some hours before that scene, I went into a café, heard a voice, and it was as if God had thrown a pebble into that place. The waves of energy touched both me and a man sitting in a corner painting a portrait. He felt the vibrations of that pebble, and so did I. So what now?

The painter knows when he has found a model. The musician knows when his instrument is well tuned. Here, in my diary, I am aware that there are certain phrases which are not written by me, but by a woman full of 'light'; I am that woman though I refuse to accept it.

I could carry on like this, but I could also, like the duck on the lake, have fun and take pleasure in that sudden ripple that set the water rocking.

There is a name for that pebble: passion. It can be used to describe the beauty of an earth-shaking meeting between two people, but it isn't just that. It's there in the excitement of the unexpected, in the desire to do something with real fervour, in the certainty that one is going to realise a dream. Passion sends us signals that guide us through our lives, and it's up to me to interpret those signs.

I would like to believe that I'm in love. With someone I don't know and who didn't figure in my plans at all. All these months of self-control, of denying love, have had exactly the opposite result: I have let myself be swept away by the first person to treat me a little differently.

It's just as well I don't have his phone number, that I don't know where he lives; that way I can lose him without having to blame myself for another missed opportunity.

And if that is what happens, if I have already lost him, I will at least have gained one very happy day in my life. Considering the way the world is, one happy day is almost a miracle.

When she arrived at the Copacabana that night, he was there, waiting for her. He was the only customer. Milan, who had been following her life with some interest, saw that she had lost the battle.

'Would you like a drink?' the man asked.

'I have to work. I can't risk losing my job.'

'I'm here as a customer. I'm making a professional proposition.'

This man, who had seemed so sure of himself that afternoon in the café, who wielded a paintbrush with such skill, met important people, had an agent in Barcelona and doubtless earned a lot of money, was now revealing his fragility; he had entered a world he should not have entered; he was no longer in a romantic café on the road to Santiago. The charm of the afternoon vanished.

'So, would you like a drink?'

'I will another time. I have clients waiting for me tonight.'

Milan overheard these last words; he was wrong, she had not allowed herself to be caught in the trap of promises of love. He nevertheless wondered, at the end of a rather slack night, why she had preferred the company of an old man, a dull accountant and an insurance salesman ...

Oh, well, it was her problem. As long as she paid her commission, it wasn't up to him to decide who she should or shouldn't go to bed with.

From Maria's diary, after that night with the old man, the accountant and the insurance salesman:

What does this painter want of me? Doesn't he realise that we are from different countries, cultures and sexes? Does he think I know more about pleasure than he does and wants to learn something from me?

Why didn't he say anything else to me, apart from 'I'm here as a customer'? It would have been so easy for him to say: 'I missed you' or 'I really enjoyed the afternoon we spent together'. I would respond in the same way (I'm a professional), but he should understand my insecurities, because I'm a woman, I'm fragile, and when I'm in that place, I'm a different person.

He's a man. He's an artist. He should know that the great aim of every human being is to understand the meaning of total love. Love is not to be found in someone else, but in ourselves; we simply awaken it. But in order to do that, we need the other person. The universe only makes sense when we have someone to share our feelings with.

He says he's tired of sex. So am I, and yet neither of us really knows what that means. We are allowing one of the most important things in life to die – he should have saved me, I should have saved him, but he left me no choice.

She was terrified. She was beginning to realise that after long months of self-control, the pressure, the earthquake, the volcano of her soul was showing signs that it was about to erupt, and the moment that this happened, she would have no way of controlling her feelings. Who was this wretched painter, who might well be lying about his life and with whom she had spent only a few hours, who had not touched her or tried to seduce her – could there be anything worse?

Why were alarm bells ringing in her heart? Because she sensed that the same thing was happening to him, but no, she must be wrong. Ralf Hart just wanted to find a woman capable of awakening in him the fire that had almost burned out; he wanted to make her into some kind of personal sex goddess, with her 'special light' (he was being honest about that), who would take him by the hand and show him the road back to life. He couldn't imagine that Maria felt the same indifference, that she had her own problems (even after so many men, she had still never achieved orgasm when having ordinary penetrative sex), that she had been making plans that very morning and was organising a triumphant return to her homeland.

Why was she thinking about him? Why was she thinking about someone who, at that very moment, might be painting another woman, saying that she had a 'special light', that she could be his sex goddess?

'I'm thinking about him because I was able to talk to him.'

How ridiculous! Did she think about the librarian? No. Did she think about Nyah, the Filipino girl, the only one of all the women who worked at the Copacabana with whom she could share some of her feelings? No, she didn't. And they were people with whom she had often talked and with whom she felt comfortable.

She tried to divert her attention to thoughts of how hot it was, or to the supermarket she hadn't managed to get to yesterday. She wrote a long letter to her father, full of details about the piece of land she would like to buy – that would make her family happy. She did not give a date for her return, but she hinted that it would be soon. She slept, woke up, slept again and woke again. She realised that the book about farming was fine for Swiss farmers, but completely useless for Brazilians – they were two entirely different worlds.

As the afternoon wore on, she noticed that the earthquake, the volcano, the pressure was diminishing. She felt more relaxed; this kind of sudden passion had happened before and had always subsided by the next day – good, her universe continued unchanged. She had a family who loved her, a man who was waiting for her and who now wrote to her frequently, telling her that the draper's shop was expanding. Even if she decided to get on a plane that night, she had enough money to buy a small farm. She had got through the worst part, the language barrier, the loneliness, the first night in the restaurant with that Arab man, the way in which she had persuaded her soul not to complain about what she was doing with her body. She knew what her dream was and she was prepared to do anything to achieve it. And that dream did not, by the way, include men, at least not men who didn't speak her mother tongue or live in her hometown.

When the earthquake had subsided, Maria realised she was partly to blame. Why had she not said to him: 'I'm lonely, I'm as miserable as you are, yesterday you saw my "light", and it was the first nice, honest thing a man has said to me since I got here.'

On the radio they were playing an old song: 'my loves die even before they're born'. Yes, that was what happened with her, that was her fate.

From Maria's diary, two days after everything had returned to normal:

Passion makes a person stop eating, sleeping, working, feeling at peace. A lot of people are frightened because, when it appears, it demolishes all the old things it finds in its path.

No one wants their life thrown into chaos. That is why a lot of people keep that threat under control, and are somehow capable of sustaining a house or a structure that is already rotten. They are the engineers of the superseded.

Other people think exactly the opposite: they surrender themselves without a second thought, hoping to find in passion the solutions to all their problems. They make the other person responsible for their happiness and blame them for their possible unhappiness. They are either euphoric because something marvellous has happened or depressed because something unexpected has just ruined everything.

Keeping passion at bay or surrendering blindly to it – which of these two attitudes is the least destructive?

I don't know.

On the third day, as if risen from the dead, Ralf Hart returned, almost too late, for Maria was already talking to another customer. When she saw him, though, she politely told the other man that she didn't want to dance, that she was waiting for someone else.

Only then did she realise that she had spent the last three days waiting for him. And at that moment, she accepted everything that fate had placed in her path.

She didn't get angry with herself; she was happy, she could allow herself that luxury, because one day she would leave this city; she knew this love was impossible, and yet, expecting nothing, she could nevertheless have everything she still hoped for from that particular stage in her life.

Ralf asked her if she would like a drink, and Maria asked for a fruit juice cocktail. The owner of the bar, pretending that he was washing glasses, stared uncomprehendingly at her: what had made her change her mind? He hoped they wouldn't just sit there drinking, and felt relieved when Ralf asked her to dance. They were following the ritual; there was no reason to feel worried.

Maria felt Ralf's hand on her waist, his cheek pressed to hers, and the music – thank God – was too loud for them to talk. One fruit juice cocktail wasn't enough to give her courage, and the few words they had exchanged had been very formal. Now it was just a question of time: would they go to a hotel? Would they make love? It shouldn't be difficult,

123

since he had already said that he wasn't interested in sex – it would just be a matter of going through the motions. On the other hand, that lack of interest would help to kill off any vestige of potential passion – she didn't know now why she had put herself through such torment after their first meeting.

Tonight she would be the Understanding Mother. Ralf Hart was just another desperate man, like millions of others. If she played her role well, if she managed to follow the rules she had laid down for herself since she began working at the Copacabana, there was no reason to worry. It was very dangerous, though, having that man so near, now that she could smell him – and she liked the way he smelled – now that she could feel his touch – and she liked his touch – now that she realised she had been waiting for him – she did not like that.

Within forty-five minutes they had fulfilled all the rules, and the man went over to the owner of the bar and said:

'I'm going to spend the rest of the night with her. I'll pay you as if I were three clients.'

The owner shrugged and thought again that the Brazilian girl would end up falling into the trap of love. Maria, for her part, was surprised: she hadn't realised that Ralf Hart knew the rules so well.

'Let's go back to my house.'

Perhaps that was the best thing to do, she thought. Although it went against all of Milan's advice, she decided, in this case, to make an exception. Apart from finding out once and for all whether or not he was married, she would also find out how famous painters live, and one day she would be able to write an article for her local newspaper, so that everyone would know that, during her time in Europe, she had moved in intellectual and artistic circles.

'What an absurd excuse!' she thought.

Half an hour later, they arrived at a small village near Geneva, called Cologny; there was a church, a bakery, a town hall, everything in its proper place. And he really did live in a two-storey house, not an apartment! First reaction: he really must be rich. Second reaction: if he were married, he wouldn't dare to do this, because they would be bound to be seen by someone.

So, he was rich and single.

They went into a hall from which a staircase ascended to the second floor, but they went straight ahead to the two rooms at the back that looked onto the garden. There was a dining table in one of the rooms, and the walls were crowded with paintings. In the other room were sofas and chairs, packed bookshelves, overflowing ashtrays and dirty glasses that had clearly been there for a long time.

'Would you like a coffee?'

Maria shook her head. No, she wouldn't. You can't treat me differently just yet. I'm confronting my own demons, doing exactly the opposite of what I promised myself I would do. But let's take things slowly; tonight I'll play the part of prostitute or friend or Understanding Mother, even though in my soul I'm a Daughter in need of affection. When it's all over, then you can make me a coffee.

'At the bottom of the garden is my studio, my soul. Here, amongst all these paintings and books, is my brain, what I think.'

125

Maria thought of her own apartment. She had no garden at the back. She did not even have any books, apart from those she borrowed from the library, since there was no point in spending money on something she could get for free. There were no paintings either, apart from a poster for the Shanghai Acrobatic Circus, which she dreamed of going to one day.

Ralf picked up a bottle of whisky and offered her a glass.

'No, thank you.'

He poured himself a drink and swallowed it down in one – without ice, without time to savour it. He started talking about intelligent things, but, however interesting the conversation, she knew that he too was afraid of what was going to happen, now that they were alone. Maria had regained control of the situation.

Ralf poured himself another whisky and, as if he were making some utterly inconsequential remark, he said:

'I need you.'

A pause. A long silence. Don't help to break that silence, let's see what he does next.

'I need you, Maria. Because you have a light, although I don't really think you believe me yet, and think I'm just trying to seduce you with my words. Don't ask me: "Why me? What's so special about me?" There isn't anything special about you, at least, nothing I can put my finger on. And yet – and here's the mystery of life – I can't think of anything else.'

'I wasn't going to ask you,' she lied.

'If I were looking for an explanation, I would say: the woman in front of me has managed to overcome suffering and to transform it into something positive, something creative, but that doesn't explain everything.'

126

It was becoming difficult to escape. He went on:

'And what about me? I have my creativity, I have my paintings, which are sought after by galleries all over the world, I have realised my dream, my village thinks of me as a beloved son, my ex-wives never ask me for alimony or anything like that, I have good health, reasonable looks, everything a man could want ... And yet here I am saying to a woman I met in a café and with whom I have spent one afternoon: "I need you." Do you know what loneliness is?'

'I do.'

'But you don't know what loneliness is like when you have the chance to be with other people all the time, when you get invitations every night to parties, cocktail parties, opening nights at the theatre ... When women are always ringing you up, women who love your work, who say how much they would like to have supper with you – they're beautiful, intelligent, educated women. But something pushes you away and says: "Don't go. You won't enjoy yourself. You'll spend the whole night trying to impress them and squander your energies proving to yourself how you can charm the whole world."'

'So I stay at home, go into my studio and try to find the light I saw in you, and I can only see that light when I'm working.'

'What can I give you that you don't already have?' she asked, feeling slightly humiliated by that remark about other women, but remembering that he had, after all, paid to have her at his side.

He drank a third glass of whisky. Maria accompanied him in her imagination, the alcohol burning his throat and his stomach, entering his bloodstream and filling him with courage, and she too began to feel drunk, even though she hadn't touched a drop. When Ralf spoke again, his voice sounded steadier:

'I can't buy your love, but you did tell me that you knew everything about sex. Teach me, then. Or teach me something about Brazil. Anything, just as long as I can be with you.'

What next?

'I only know two places in my own country: the town I was born in and Rio de Janeiro. As for sex, I don't think I can teach you anything. I'm nearly twenty-three, you're about six years older, but I know you've lived life very intensely. I know men who pay me to do what they want, not what I want.'

'I've done everything a man could dream of doing with one, two, even three women at the same time. And I don't think I learned very much.'

Silence again, except that this time it was Maria's turn to speak. And he did not help her, just as she had not helped him before.

'Do you want me as a professional?'

'I want you however you want to be wanted.'

No, he couldn't have said that, because that was precisely what she had wanted to hear. The earthquake, the volcano, the storm returned. It was going to be impossible to escape her own trap, she would lose this man without ever really having him.

'You know what I mean, Maria. Teach me. Perhaps that will save me, perhaps it will save you and bring us both back to life. You're right, I am only six years older than you, and

128

yet I've lived enough for several lives. Our experiences have been entirely different, but we are both desperate people; the only thing that brings us any peace is being together.'

Why was he saying these things? It wasn't possible, and yet it was true. They had only met once before and yet they already needed each other. Imagine what would happen if they continued seeing each other; it would be disastrous! Maria was an intelligent woman, with many months behind her now of reading and of observing humankind; she had an aim in life, but she also had a soul, which she needed to know in order to discover her 'light'. She was becoming tired of being who she was, and although her imminent return to Brazil was an interesting challenge, she had not yet learned all she could. Ralf Hart was a man who had accepted challenges and had learned everything, and now he was asking this woman, this prostitute, this Understanding Mother, to save him. How absurd!

Other men had behaved like this with her. Many of them had been unable to have an erection, others had wanted to be treated like children, others had said that they would like her to be their wife because it excited them to know that she had had so many lovers. Although she had still not met any of the 'special clients', she had already discovered the vast universe of fantasies that fills the human soul. But they were all used to their own worlds and none of them had said to her: 'take me away from here'. On the contrary, they wanted to take Maria with them.

And even though those many men had always left her with money, but drained of energy, she must have learned something. If one of them had really been looking for love,

129

and if sex really was only part of that search, how would she like to be treated? What did she think should happen on a first meeting?

What would she really like to happen?

'I'd like a gift,' said Maria.

Ralf Hart didn't understand. A gift? He had already paid for that night in advance, while they were in the taxi, because he knew the ritual. What did she mean?

Maria had suddenly realised that she knew, at that moment, what a man and a woman needed to feel. She took his hand and led him into one of the sitting rooms.

'We won't go up to the bedroom,' she said.

She turned out almost all the lights, sat down on the carpet and asked him to sit down opposite her. She noticed that there was a fire in the room.

'Light the fire.'

'But it's summer.'

'Light the fire. You asked me to guide our steps tonight and that's what I'm doing.'

She gave him a steady look, hoping that he would again see her 'light'. He obviously did, because he went out into the garden, collected some wood still wet with rain, and picked up some old newspapers so that the fire would dry the wood and get it to burn. He went into the kitchen to fetch more whisky, but Maria called him back.

'Did you ask me what I wanted?'

'No, I didn't.'

'Well, the person you're with has to exist too. Think of her. Think if she wants whisky or gin or coffee. Ask her what she wants.'

'What would you like to drink.'

'Wine. And I'd like you to keep me company.'

He put down the whisky bottle and returned with a bottle of wine. By this time, the fire was already beginning to burn; Maria turned out the few remaining lights, so that the flames were the only illumination in the room. She behaved as if she had always known that this was the first step: recognising the other person and knowing that he or she was there.

She opened her handbag and found inside a pen she had bought in a supermarket. Anything would do.

'This is for you. I bought it so that I could note down some ideas about farm management. I used it for two days, I worked until I was too tired to work any more. It contains some of my sweat, some of my concentration and my willpower, and I'm giving it to you now.'

She placed the pen gently in his hand.

'Instead of buying something that you would like to have, I'm giving you something that is mine, truly mine. A gift. A sign of respect for the person before me, asking him to understand how important it is to be by his side. Now he has a small part of me with him, which I gave him with my free, spontaneous will.'

Ralf got up, went over to a shelf and returned, carrying something. He held it out to Maria.

'This is a carriage belonging to an electric train set I had when I was a child. I wasn't allowed to play with it on my own, because my father said it had been imported from the United States and was very expensive. So I had to wait until he felt like setting up the train in the living room, but he spent most Sundays listening to opera. That's why the train survived my childhood, but never gave me any happiness. I've still got all the track, the engine, the houses, even the manual, because I had a train that wasn't mine and with which I never played.

'I wish I'd destroyed it along with all the other toys I was given and which I've since forgotten all about, because that passion for destruction is part of how a child discovers the world. But this pristine train set always reminds me of a part of my childhood that I never lived, because it was too precious and it meant too much work for my father. Or perhaps it was just that whenever he set the train up, he was afraid he might show his love for me.'

Maria began staring into the fire. Something was happening, and it wasn't just the wine or the cosy atmosphere. It was that exchange of gifts.

Ralf turned to the fire too. They said nothing, listening to the crackle of the flames. They drank their wine, as if it didn't matter that they said nothing, did nothing. They were just there, together, staring in the same direction.

'I have a lot of pristine train sets in my life too,' said Maria, after a while. 'One of them is my heart. And I only played with it when the world set out the tracks, and then it wasn't always the right moment.'

'But you loved.'

'Oh, yes, I loved, I loved very deeply. I loved so deeply that when my love asked me for a gift, I took fright and fled.'

'I don't understand.'

'You don't have to. I'm teaching you because I've discovered something I didn't know before. The giving of gifts. Giving something of one's own. Giving something important rather than asking. You have my treasure: the pen with which I wrote down some of my dreams. I have your treasure: the carriage of a train, part of your childhood that you did not live.

'I carry with me part of your past, and you carry with you a little of my present. Isn't that lovely?'

She said all this without blinking, and without surprise, as if she had known for ages that this was the best and only way to behave. She got lightly to her feet, took her jacket from the coat rack and kissed Ralf on the cheek. Ralf Hart did not make any move to get up, hypnotised by the fire, perhaps thinking about his father.

'I never understood why I kept that carriage. Now I do: it was in order to give it to you one night before an open fire. Now the house feels lighter.'

He said that the next day he would give the rest of the tracks, engines, smoke pills, to some children's home.

'It could be a rarity, of a kind that isn't made any more; it could be worth a lot of money,' said Maria, but immediately regretted her words. That wasn't what mattered, the point was to free yourself from something that cost your heart even more.

Before she said anything else that did not quite chime with the moment, she again kissed him on the cheek and walked to the front door. He was still gazing into the fire, and she had to ask him softly if he would open the door for her.

Ralf got up, and she explained that, although she was glad to see him staring into the fire, Brazilians have a strange superstition: when you visit someone for the first time, you must not be the one to open the door when you leave, because if you do, you will never return to that house.

'And I want to come back.'

'Although we didn't take our clothes off and I didn't come inside you, or even touch you, we've made love.'

She laughed. He offered to take her home, but she refused.

'I'll come and see you tomorrow, then, at the Copacabana.'

'No, don't. Wait a week. I've learned that waiting is the most difficult bit, and I want to get used to the feeling, knowing that you're with me, even when you're not by my side.'

She walked back through the cold and the dark, as she had so many times before in Geneva; normally, these walks were associated with sadness, loneliness, the desire to go back to Brazil, financial calculations, timetables, nostalgia for the language she hadn't spoken freely for ages.

Now, though, she was walking in order to find herself, to find that woman who had sat with a man by a fire for forty minutes and who was full of light, wisdom, experience and charm. She had seen that woman's face a long time ago, when she was walking by the lakeside wondering whether or not she should devote herself to a life that wasn't hers – on that afternoon, the woman had a terribly sad smile on her face. She had seen her for a second time on that folded canvas, and now she was with her again. She only caught a taxi after she had walked quite a way, when the magic presence had gone, leaving her alone again, as usual.

It was best not to think too much about it all, so as not to spoil it, so as not to let the beauty of what she had just experienced be replaced by anxiety. If that other Maria really existed, she would return when the moment was right.

An extract from the diary Maria wrote on the night she was given the train carriage:

Profound desire, true desire is the desire to be close to someone. From that point onwards, things change, the man and the woman come into play, but what happens before – the attraction that brought them together – is impossible to explain. It is untouched desire in its purest state.

When desire is still in this pure state, the man and the woman fall in love with life, they live each moment reverently, consciously, always ready to celebrate the next blessing.

When people feel like this, they are not in a hurry, they do not precipitate events with unthinking actions. They know that the inevitable will happen, that what is real always finds a way of revealing itself. When the moment comes, they do not hesitate, they do not miss an opportunity, they do not let slip a single magic moment, because they respect the importance of each second.

In the days that followed, Maria found herself once more caught in the trap she had tried so hard to avoid, but she felt neither sad nor concerned. On the contrary, now that she had nothing to lose, she was free.

She knew that, however romantic the situation, one day, Ralf Hart would realise that she was just a prostitute, while he was a respected artist, that she lived in a far-off country that was in a state of permanent crisis, while he lived in paradise, with his life organised and protected from birth. He had received his education in the best schools, museums and art galleries of the world, while she had barely finished secondary school. Dreams like theirs never lasted long, and Maria had enough experience of life to know that reality usually chose not to fit in with her dreams. And that was now her great joy: to say to reality that she didn't need it, that she was no longer dependent on what happened in order to be happy.

'God, I'm such a romantic.'

During the week, she tried to think of something that would make Ralf Hart happy; for he had restored to her a dignity and a 'light' that she thought were lost forever. But the only way she had of repaying him was with the thing he thought was her speciality: sex. Since there was little to inspire her in the routine at the Copacabana, she decided to look elsewhere.

She again went to see a few porn movies, and again found nothing of interest in them, apart, perhaps, from the varying number of people involved. When films proved of no help, she decided, for the first time since she had arrived in Geneva, to buy some books, although she still didn't see the point in cluttering up her apartment with something which, once read, had no further use. She went to the bookshop she had seen when she and Ralf had walked down the road to Santiago, and asked if they had any books about sex.

'Oh, loads,' said the shop assistant. 'In fact, it seems to be all people care about. There's a special section devoted to the subject, but in just about every other novel you can see around you there's always at least one sex scene. Whether it's hidden away in pretty little love stories or discussed in serious tomes on human behaviour, it appears to be all anyone thinks about.'

Maria, with all her experience, knew that the woman was wrong: people wanted to think like that because they thought sex was everyone else's sole concern. They went on diets, wore wigs, spent hours at the hairdresser's or at the gym, put on sexy clothes, all in an attempt to awaken the necessary spark. And what happened? When the moment came to go to bed with someone, eleven minutes later it was all over. There was no creativity involved, nothing that would lift them up to paradise; the fire provoked by the spark soon burned out.

But there was no point arguing with the young blonde woman, who believed that the world could be explained in books. She asked to be directed to the special section, and there she found various books about gay men, lesbians, nuns revealing scandals in the church, illustrated books showing oriental techniques, all involving extremely uncomfortable positions, but only one of the titles interested her: *Sacred Sex*. At least it was different.

She bought it, went home, tuned to a particular radio station that always helped her to think (because they played such calming music), opened the book and noticed various illustrations, showing postures that only a circus performer could possibly hope to achieve. The text itself was very dull.

Maria had learned enough in her profession to know that not everything in life is a matter of what position you adopt when making love, and that any variation usually occurs naturally, without thinking, like the steps in a dance. Nevertheless, she tried to concentrate on what she was reading.

Two hours later, she had come to two conclusions.

First, she needed to eat supper, because she had to get back to the Copacabana.

Second, the person who had written the book clearly understood nothing, absolutely nothing about the subject. It was just a lot of empty theory, oriental nonsense, pointless rituals and idiotic suggestions. She noticed that the author had studied meditation in the Himalayas (she must find out where they were), attended courses in yoga (she had heard of that), and had obviously read widely in the subject, for she kept quoting other authors, but she had failed to learn what was essential. Sex wasn't theories, incense, erogenous zones, bows and salaams. How did that person (a woman) have the nerve to write on a subject which not even Maria, who worked in the field, knew in depth. Perhaps it was all the fault of the Himalayas or the need to complicate something whose very beauty lay in simplicity and passion. If that woman could get away with publishing and selling such a stupid book, perhaps she should think seriously again about writing her own: *Eleven Minutes*. It wouldn't be cynical or false – it would just be her story.

But she had neither the time nor the interest; she needed to focus her energies on making Ralf Hart happy and on learning how to manage a farm.

From Maria's diary, just after abandoning the boring book:

I've met a man and fallen in love with him. I allowed myself to fall in love for one simple reason: I'm not expecting anything to come of it. I know that, in three months' time, I'll be far away and he'll be just a memory, but I couldn't stand living without love any longer; I had reached my limit.

I'm writing a story for Ralf Hart – that's his name. I'm not sure he'll come back to the club where I work, but, for the first time in my life, that doesn't matter. It's enough just to love him, to be with him in my thoughts and to colour this lovely city with his steps, his words, his love. When I leave this country, it will have a face and a name and the memory of a fireplace. Everything else I experienced here, all the difficulties I had to overcome, will be as nothing compared to that memory.

I would like to do for him what he did for me. I've been thinking about it a lot, and I realise that I didn't go into that café by chance; really important meetings are planned by the souls long before the bodies see each other.

Generally speaking, these meetings occur when we reach a limit, when we need to die and be reborn emotionally. These meetings are waiting for us, but more often than not, we avoid them happening. If we are desperate, though, if we have nothing to lose, or if we are full of enthusiasm for life, then the unknown reveals itself, and our universe changes direction.

Everyone knows how to love, because we are all born with that gift. Some people have a natural talent for it, but the majority of us have to re-learn, to remember how to love, and everyone, without exception, needs to burn on the bonfire of past emotions, to relive certain joys and griefs, certain ups and downs, until they can see the connecting thread that exists behind each new encounter; because there is a connecting thread.

And then, our bodies learn to speak the language of the soul, known as sex, and that is what I can give to the man who gave me back my soul, even though he has no idea how important he is to my life. That is what he asked me for and that is what he will have; I want him to be very happy.

Sometimes life is very mean: a person can spend days, weeks, months and years without feeling anything new. Then, when a door opens – as happened with Maria when she met Ralf Hart – a positive avalanche pours in. One moment, you have nothing, the next, you have more than you can cope with.

Two hours after writing her diary, when she arrived at work, Milan, the owner, came looking for her:

'So you went out with that painter, did you?'

Ralf was obviously known at the club – she had realised this when he paid the rate for three customers, without having to ask the price. Maria merely nodded, trying to act mysterious, but Milan took no notice; he knew this life better than she did.

'Perhaps you're ready for the next stage. There's a special client of ours who has often asked about you. I told him that you're not experienced enough, and he believed me, but perhaps now is the moment to try.'

A special client?

'What's this got to do with the painter?'

'He's a special client too.'

So everything she had done with Ralf Hart had already been done by one of her colleagues. She bit her lip and said nothing; she had had a lovely week, and she must not forget what she had written.

'Should I do the same thing I did with him?'

'I don't know what you did; but tonight, if someone offers you a drink, say no. Special clients pay more; you won't regret it.'

Work started as it always did. The Thai women all sat together, the Colombians adopted their usual air of knowing everything, the three Brazilians (including her) looked absently about them, as if nothing could ever surprise or interest them. Apart from them, there was an Austrian, two Germans, and the rest were tall, pretty women with pale eyes who came from the former Eastern Bloc countries and who always seemed to find husbands more quickly than the others.

The men began to arrive – Russian, Swiss, German, all of them busy executives, well able to afford the services of the most expensive prostitutes in one of the most expensive cities in the world. Some came over to her table, but she kept her eye on Milan, who shook his head. Maria was pleased; tonight, she wouldn't have to open her legs, put up with smells or take showers in sometimes chilly bathrooms; all she had to do was to teach a man grown weary of sex how to make love. And when she thought about it, not every woman would have been creative enough to come up with that story about the exchange of gifts.

At the same time, she was wondering: Why is it that, having experienced everything, these men want to go right back to the start? Not that this was her concern; as long as they paid well, she was there to serve them.

A man came in, younger than Ralf Hart; he was good-looking, with dark hair, perfect teeth, and wearing what looked like a Mao jacket – no tie, just a high collar and, underneath, an impeccable white shirt. He went up to the bar, where both he and Milan turned to look at Maria; then he came over.

'Would you like a drink?'

She saw Milan nod, and so invited the man to sit down at her table. She ordered a fruit juice cocktail and waited for him to ask her to dance. Then the man introduced himself:

'My name is Terence, and I work for a record company in England. Since I assume I'm in a place where I can trust the personnel, I take it this will remain entirely between you and me.'

Maria was about to start talking about Brazil, but he interrupted her:

'Milan says you understand what I want.'

'I've no idea what you want, but I know my job.'

They did not follow the usual ritual; he paid the bill, took her arm and they got into a taxi, where he gave her a thousand francs. For a moment, she remembered the Arab man with whom she had gone to the restaurant full of famous paintings; it was the first time she had received the same amount of money, and instead of making her feel glad, it made her feel nervous.

The taxi stopped outside one of the most expensive hotels in the city. The man greeted the porter and seemed totally at ease in the place. They went straight up to his room, a suite with a view over the river. He opened a bottle of wine – possibly a rare vintage – and offered her a glass.

Maria watched him while he drank; what did a rich, good-looking man like him want with a prostitute? Since he barely spoke, she too remained largely silent, trying to work out what would make a special client happy. She knew that she should not take the initiative, but once the process had begun, she needed to be able to follow his lead as quickly as possible; after all, it wasn't every night that she earned a thousand francs.

'We've got plenty of time,' Terence said. 'All the time in the world. You can sleep here if you like.'

Her feelings of insecurity returned. The man did not seem in the least intimidated, and, unlike her other customers, he spoke very calmly. He knew what he wanted; he put on the perfect piece of music, at the perfect volume, in the perfect room, with the perfect window, which looked out onto the lake of a perfect city. His suit was welltailored, his suitcase was there in the corner, very small, as if he always travelled light, or as if he had come to Geneva just for that one night.

'I'll sleep at home,' Maria said.

The man opposite her changed completely. An icy glint came into his hitherto gentlemanly eyes.

'Sit there,' he said, indicating a chair by the desk.

It was an order! A real order. Maria obeyed and, oddly enough, she felt excited.

'Sit properly. Back straight, like a lady. If you don't, I'll punish you.'

Punish her! Special client! In a flash, she understood everything, took the thousand francs out of her bag and put it down on the desk.

'I know what you want,' she said, looking deep into those cold, blue eyes. 'And I won't do it.'

The man seemed to return to his normal self and he could see that she was telling the truth.

'Have a drink of wine,' he said. 'I won't force you to do anything. You can either stay a little longer, if you like, or you can leave.'

That made her feel better.

'I have a job. I have a boss who protects and trusts me. I'd be grateful if you didn't say anything to him.'

Maria said this without a hint of pleading or self-pity in her voice; it was simply how things were.

Terence was once again the man she had first met – neither gentle nor harsh, just someone who, unlike her other clients, gave the impression that he knew what he wanted. He seemed to emerge from a trance, from a play that had scarcely begun.

Was it worth leaving now and never finding out the truth about this 'special client'?

'What exactly did you want?'

'You know what I want. Pain. Suffering. And a great deal of pleasure.'

'Pain and suffering don't normally go with pleasure,' Maria thought. And yet she desperately wanted to believe that they did, and thus make a positive out of her many negative experiences.

He took her by the hand and led her over to the window: on the other side of the lake they could see a cathedral spire. Maria remembered passing it when she had walked the road to Santiago with Ralf Hart.

'You see the river, the lake, the houses and the church? Well, it was all pretty much the same five hundred years ago, except that the city was deserted. A strange disease had spread throughout Europe, and no one knew why so many people were dying. They began to call the disease the Black Death – sent by God because of mankind's sins.

'Then a group of people decided to sacrifice themselves for the sake of humanity. They offered the thing they most feared: physical pain. They began to spend days and nights walking across these bridges, along these streets, beating their own bodies with whips and chains. They were suffering in the name of God and praising God with their pain. They soon realised that they were happier doing this than baking bread, working in the fields or feeding their animals. Pain was no longer a cause of suffering, but a source of pleasure because they were redeeming humanity from its sins. Pain became joy, the meaning of life, pleasure.'

His eyes grew cold again. He picked up the money she had put down on the desk, separated out one hundred and fifty francs and put those in her bag.

'Don't worry about your boss. Here's his commission, and I promise I won't say anything. You can leave now.'

She grabbed the money back.

'No!'

It was the wine, the Arab man in the restaurant, the woman with the sad smile, the idea that she would never ever return to this wretched place, the fear of a new love that was coming to her in the shape of a man, the letters to her mother telling of a wonderful life full of job opportunities, the boy from her childhood who had asked her for a pencil, the struggles with herself, the guilt, the curiosity, the money, the search to discover her own limits, and all the missed chances and opportunities. Another Maria was there now:

she was no longer offering gifts, she was offering herself up as a sacrifice.

'I'm not afraid any more. Let's carry on. If necessary, you can punish me for my rebelliousness. I've lied and betrayed and maligned the very person who protected and loved me.'

She was entering into the spirit of the game. She was saying the right things.

'Kneel down!' said Terence in a low, chilling voice.

Maria obeyed. She had never been treated this way, and she didn't know if it was good or bad, only that she wanted to go forward; she deserved to be humiliated for all she had done in her life. She was entering a role, becoming a different person, a woman she did not know at all.

'You will be punished because you are useless, because you don't know the rules and because you know nothing about sex, life or love.'

While he was speaking, Terence was transformed into two very different men. The one who was calmly explaining the rules to her and the one who made her feel like the most miserable wretch in the world.

'Do you know why I am doing this? Because there is no greater pleasure than that of initiating someone into an unknown world. Taking someone's virginity – the virginity not of their body, but of their soul, you understand.'

She understood.

'Today you can ask questions, but the next time, when the theatre curtain goes up, the play will begin and cannot be stopped. If it does stop, it is because our souls are incompatible. Remember: it is a play. You must be the person you have never had the courage to be. Gradually, you will discover that you are that person, but until you can see this clearly, you must pretend and invent.'

'What if I can't stand the pain?'

'There is no pain, only something that transforms itself into delight and mystery. It forms part of the play to say: "Don't treat me like that, you're really hurting me." As is: "Stop, I can't take any more!" In order to avoid danger ...'

He broke off at this point and said: 'Keep your head down; don't look at me!'

Maria, kneeling, lowered her head and stared at the floor.

'... in order to avoid this relationship causing any serious physical harm, we have two code words. If one of us says "yellow", that means that the violence should be decreased slightly. If one of us says "red", it must be stopped at once.'

'You said "one of us" ...'

'We take turns. One cannot exist without the other; no one can know how to humiliate another person if they themselves have not experienced humiliation.'

These were terrible words, from a world she did not know, full of shadow, slime and putrefaction. Nevertheless, she wanted to go on – her body was trembling with fear and excitement.

Terence placed his hand on her head with unexpected tenderness.

'That's all.'

He asked her to get up, not particularly kindly, but not with the same brusque aggression he had shown before. Still trembling, Maria put on her jacket. Terence noticed the state she was in.

'Have a cigarette before you go.'

'Nothing happened.'

'It doesn't need to. It will start to happen in your soul, and the next time we meet, you will be ready.'

'Was tonight worth one thousand francs?'

He didn't reply. He too lit a cigarette and they finished the wine, listening to the perfect music, savouring the silence together, until the moment came to say something, and when it did, Maria was surprised by her own words.

'I don't understand why I want to step into this slime.'

'One thousand francs.'

'No, that's not the reason.'

Terence seemed pleased with this response.

'I've asked myself the same thing. The Marquis de Sade said that the most important experiences a man can have are those that take him to the very limit; that is the only way we learn, because it requires all our courage. When a boss humiliates an employee, or a man humiliates his wife, he is merely being cowardly or taking his revenge on life, they are people who have never dared to look into the depths of their soul, never attempted to know the origin of that desire to unleash the wild beast, or to understand that sex, pain and love are all extreme experiences.

'Only those who know those frontiers know life; everything else is just passing the time, repeating the same tasks, growing old and dying without ever having discovered what we are doing here.'

In the street again, in the cold again, and again that desire to walk. The man was wrong, it wasn't necessary to know your own demons in order to find God. She passed a group of

151

students coming out of a bar; they were all happy and slightly tipsy, they were all good-looking and bursting with health; soon they would finish university and start what people call 'real life'. Work, marriage, children, television, bitterness, old age, the sense of having lost many things, frustrations, illness, disability, dependence on others, loneliness, death.

What was happening? She too was looking for the peace in which to live her 'real life'; the time spent in Switzerland, doing something she had never dreamed of doing, was just a difficult phase, the kind of thing everyone goes through at some time or another. During this difficult phase, she frequented the Copacabana, went with men for money, played the Innocent Girl, the Femme Fatale and the Understanding Mother, depending on the client. But it was just a job, which she did with total professionalism – for the sake of the tips – and minimum interest – for fear she might get used to it. She had spent the last nine months controlling the world around her, and shortly before she was due to go back to her own country, she was finding that she was capable of loving without demanding anything in return and of suffering for no reason. It was as if life had chosen this strange, sordid way of teaching her something about her own mysteries, her light and her darkness.

From Maria's diary on the night following her first meeting with Terence:

He quoted the Marquis de Sade, of whom I know nothing, apart from the word 'sadism'. It's true that we only know each other when we come up against our own limits, but it's wrong too, because it isn't necessary to know everything about ourselves; human beings weren't made solely to go in search of wisdom, but also to plough the land, wait for rain, plant the wheat, harvest the grain, make the bread.

I am two women: one wants to have all the joy, passion and adventure that life can give me. The other wants to be a slave to routine, to family life, to the things that can be planned and achieved. I'm a housewife and a prostitute, both of us living in the same body and doing battle with each other.

The meeting of these two women is a game with serious risks. A divine dance. When we meet, we are two divine energies, two universes colliding. If the meeting is not carried out with due reverence, one universe destroys the other.

She was back in Ralf Hart's living room, with the fire, the bottle of wine, the two of them sitting on the floor, and everything she had experienced the previous night with the English executive just a dream or a nightmare – depending on how she was feeling. Now she was searching once more for her reason for living, or, rather, for the kind of utter surrender by which a person offers his or her heart and asks for nothing in return.

She had grown a lot while waiting for this moment. She had finally discovered that real love has nothing to do with what she imagined, that is, with a chain of events provoked by the energy engendered by love – courtship, engagement, marriage, children, waiting, cooking, the amusement park on Sundays, more waiting, getting old together, an end to the waiting, and then, in its place, comes your husband's retirement, illnesses, the feeling that it is far too late to live out your dream together.

She looked at the man to whom she had decided to give herself, and to whom she had resolved never to reveal her feelings, because what she was feeling now was far from taking any definite form, not even physical form. He seemed more at ease, as if he were embarking on an interesting period of his life. He was smiling and telling her about his recent visit to Munich to meet an important museum director.

'He asked if the painting about the faces of Geneva was ready yet. I said I had just met one of the principal people I would like to paint, a woman who was full of light. But I don't want to talk about me, I want to embrace you. I desire you.'

Desire. Desire? Desire! That was the point of departure this evening, because it was something she knew extremely well!

For example, you awaken desire by not immediately handing over the object of that desire.

'All right, then, desire me. That's what we're doing right now. You are less than a yard away from me, you went to a nightclub, paid for my services, and you know you have the right to touch me. But you don't dare. Look at me. Look at me and imagine that perhaps I don't want you to look at me. Imagine what's hidden beneath my clothes.'

She always wore black to work, and she couldn't understand why the other girls at the Copacabana tried to look provocative in their low-cut dresses and garish colours. It seemed to her that it was more exciting for a man if she dressed like any other woman he might meet at the office, on the train or in the house of one of his wife's friends.

Ralf looked at her. Maria felt him undressing her and she enjoyed being desired like that – with no contact, as if she were in a restaurant or standing in a queue at the cinema.

'We're in a train station,' Maria went on. 'I'm standing next to you, waiting for a train, but you don't know me. My eyes meet yours, by chance, and I don't look away. You don't know what I'm trying to say, because, although you're an intelligent man, capable of seeing the "light" in other people, you are not sensitive enough to see what that light is illuminating.'

She had learned about 'theatre'. She had wanted to forget the face of that English executive as quickly as possible, but there he was, guiding her imagination.

'My eyes are fixed on yours, and I might be wondering to myself: "Do I know him from somewhere?" Or I might just be distracted. Or I might be afraid of appearing unfriendly; perhaps you do know me, and so I give you the benefit of the doubt for a few seconds, until it becomes clear either that you really do know me or that it's a case of mistaken identity.

'But I might also be wanting the simplest thing in the world: to find a man. I might be trying to escape an unhappy love affair. I might be hoping to avenge myself for a recent betrayal and have gone to the train station looking for a stranger. I might want to be your prostitute just for one night, to do something different in my otherwise boring life. I might even be a real prostitute on the look-out for work.'

A brief silence; Maria had grown distracted. She was back in that hotel room, remembering the humiliation – 'yellow', 'red', pain and a great deal of pleasure. That encounter had stirred her soul in a way she did not like at all.

Ralf noticed and tried to take her back to the train station.

'In this meeting, do you desire me too?'

'I don't know. We don't talk. You don't know.'

She grows distracted again. The 'theatre' idea is proving really very helpful; it draws out the real person and drives away the many false people who live inside us.

'The fact is that I don't look away, and you don't know what to do. Should you approach? Will you be rejected? Will I call the guard? Or invite you for a coffee perhaps?'

'I'm on my way back from Munich,' Ralf Hart said, and his voice sounds different, as if they really were meeting for the first time. 'I'm thinking about a collection of paintings on the many personalities of sex, the many masks that people wear in order never to experience a real encounter.'

He knew about the 'theatre'. Milan had said that he too was a 'special client'. An alarm bell rang, but she needed time to think.

'The director of the museum said to me: what are you going to base your work on? I said: On women who feel free enough to earn their living making love. He said: That won't work; we call such women "prostitutes". I said: Fine, they are prostitutes; I'm going to study their history and create something more intellectual, more to the taste of the families who visit your museum. It's all a question of culture, you see. Of finding a palatable way of presenting something that is otherwise very hard to take.

'The director insisted: But sex is no longer a taboo. It's been so over-exploited that it's difficult to produce any new work on the subject. I said: Do you know where sexual desire comes from? From our instinct, said the director. Yes, I said, from our instinct, but everyone knows that. How can you make a beautiful exhibition if all we are talking about is science? I want to talk about how man explains that attraction, the way, let's say, a philosopher would explain it. The director asked me to give him an example. I said that if, when I caught the train back home, a woman looked at me, I would go over and speak to her; I would say that, since we were strangers, we had the freedom to do anything we wanted, to live out all our fantasies, and then go home to our wife or husband and never meet again. And then, in the train station, I see you.'

'Your story is so interesting it's in danger of killing desire.'

Ralf Hart laughed and agreed. They had finished one bottle of wine and he went into the kitchen to fetch another; and she sat staring into the fire, knowing what the next step would be, but, at the same time, savouring the cosy atmosphere, forgetting about the English executive, and regaining that sense of surrender.

Ralf filled their two glasses, and Maria said:

'Just out of curiosity, how would you end that story with the museum director?'

'Since I was in the company of an intellectual, I would quote from Plato. According to him, at the beginning of creation, men and women were not as they are now; there was just one being, who was rather short, with a body and a neck, but his head had two faces, looking in different directions. It was as if two creatures had been glued back to back, with two sets of sex organs, four legs and four arms.

'The Greek gods, however, were jealous, because this creature with four arms could work harder; with its two faces, it was always vigilant and could not be taken by surprise; and its four legs meant that it could stand or walk for long periods at a time without tiring. Even more dangerous was the fact that the creature had two different sets of sex organs and so needed no one else in order to continue reproducing.

'Zeus, the supreme lord of Olympus, said: "I have a plan to make these mortals lose some of their strength."

'And he cut the creature in two with a lightning bolt, thus creating man and woman. This greatly increased the population of the world, and, at the same time, disoriented and weakened its inhabitants, because now they had to search for their lost half and embrace it and, in that embrace, regain their former strength, their ability to avoid betrayal and the stamina to walk for long periods of time and to withstand hard work. That embrace in which the two bodies re-fuse to become one again is what we call sex.'

'Is that a true story?'

'According to the Greek philosopher, Plato, yes.'

Maria was gazing at him, fascinated, and the experience of the previous night had vanished completely. She saw that the man before her was full of the same 'light' that he had seen in her, entirely involved in telling her that strange story, his eyes alight now not with desire but with joy.

'Can I ask you a favour?'

Ralf said she could ask anything she wanted.

'Is it possible to know why, after the gods had split the four-legged creature in two, some of them decided that the embrace could be merely a thing, just another business transaction, which instead of increasing people's energy, diminished it?'

'You mean prostitution?'

'Yes. Could you find out if, in the beginning, sex was something sacred?'

'If you like,' replied Ralf, 'although it's not something I've ever thought about, nor, as far as I know, has anyone else. Perhaps there isn't any literature on the subject.'

Maria could stand the pressure no longer:

'Has it ever occurred to you that women, in particular, prostitutes, are capable of love?'

'Yes, it has. It occurred to me on that first day, when we were sitting in the café and I saw your light. Then, when I decided to offer you a cup of coffee, I chose to believe in everything, even in the possibility of you returning me to the world I left a long, long time ago.'

There was no going back now. Maria, the teacher, needed to rush to her own aid, otherwise she would kiss him, embrace him and ask him never to leave her.

'Let's go back to the train station,' she said. 'Or, rather, let's come back to this room, to the day when we sat here together for the first time and you recognised that I existed and gave me a gift. That was your first attempt to enter my soul, and you weren't sure whether or not you were welcome. But, as you say in your story, human beings were once divided and now seek the embrace that will reunite them. That is our instinct. But it is also our reason for putting up with all the difficulties we meet in that search.

'I want you to look at me, but I want you to take care that I don't notice. Initial desire is important because it is hidden, forbidden, not permitted. You don't know whether you are looking at your lost half or not; she doesn't know either, but something is drawing you together, and you must believe that it is true you are each other's "other half".'

Where am I getting all this? I'm drawing it up from the bottom of my heart, because this is how I always wanted it to be. I'm drawing up these dreams from my own dream as a woman.

She slipped off the shoulder strap of her dress, so that one part, one tiny part of one nipple was exposed.

'Desire is not what you see, but what you imagine.'

Ralf Hart was looking at a woman with dark hair and wearing dark clothes, who was sitting on the floor of his living room, and was full of absurd desires, like having an open fire burning in the middle of summer. Yes, he would like to imagine what those clothes were hiding; he could guess the size of her breasts, and he knew that she didn't really need the bra she was wearing, although perhaps she had to wear it for her work. Her breasts were neither large nor small, they were simply young. Her eyes gave nothing away; what was she doing here? Why was he encouraging this absurd, dangerous relationship, when he had no problems finding women? He was rich, young, famous, good-looking. He loved his work; he had loved women whom he had subsequently married; he had been loved. He was someone who, according to all the rules and norms, should have been able to shout out loud: 'I'm happy.'

But he wasn't. While most of humanity was scrabbling for a piece of bread, a roof over their head and a job that would allow them to live with dignity, Ralf Hart had all of that, and it only made him feel more wretched. If he looked back on what his life had been lately, he had perhaps managed two or three days when he had woken up, looked at the sun – or the rain – and felt glad to see the morning, just happy, without wanting anything, planning anything or asking anything in exchange. Apart from those few days, the rest of his existence had been wasted on dreams, both frustrated and realised – a desire to go beyond himself, to go beyond his limitations; he had spent his life trying to prove something, but he didn't know what or to whom.

He looked at the beautiful woman before him, who was discreetly dressed in black, someone he had met by chance, although he had seen her before at the nightclub and thought that she seemed out of place. She had asked him to desire her, and he desired her intensely, far more than she could imagine, but it wasn't her breasts or her body, it was her company he desired. He wanted to put his arms around her and to sit in silence, staring into the fire, drinking wine, smoking the occasional cigarette; that would be enough. Life was made up of simple things; he was weary of all the years he had spent searching for something, though quite what he didn't know.

And yet, if he did that, if he touched her, all would be lost. For, despite the 'light' he could see in Maria, he wasn't sure she realised how good it was for him to be by her side. Was he paying? Yes, and he would continue paying for as long as it took to win her, to sit with her by the lakeside and speak of love, and to hear her say the same thing. It was best not to take any chances, not to rush things, not to say anything.

Ralf Hart stopped tormenting himself and concentrated once more on the game they had just created together. The woman before him was right; the wine, the fire, the cigarettes and the company were not enough in themselves; another kind of intoxication, another kind of flame was required.

She was wearing a dress with shoulder straps; she was revealing one breast; he could see her skin, more dark than pale. He desired her. He desired her intensely.

Maria noticed the change in Ralf's eyes. Knowing that she was desired excited her more than anything else. It had nothing to do with the automatic formula – I want to make love with you, I want to get married, I want you to have an orgasm, I want you to have my child, I want commitment. No, desire was an entirely free sensation, loose in the air, vibrating, filling life with the will to have something – and that was enough, that will carried all before it, moved mountains, made her wet.

Desire was the source of everything else – leaving her country, discovering a new world, learning French, overcoming her prejudices, dreaming of having a farm, loving without asking for anything in return, feeling that she was a woman simply because a man was looking at her. With calculated slowness, she slipped off the other strap, and the dress slid down her body. Then she undid her bra. There she was, with the upper part of her body completely bare, wondering if he would leap on her, touch her, utter vows of love, or if he was sensitive enough simply to feel sexual pleasure in desire itself.

Things around them began to change, all sound disappeared, the fire, the paintings and the books gradually vanished, to be replaced by a kind of trance-like state, in which only the object of desire exists, and nothing else is important.

The man did not move. At first, she felt a certain shyness in his eyes, but that did not last long. He was looking at her, and in the world of his imagination, he was caressing her with his tongue, they were making love, sweating, clinging to each other, mingling tenderness and violence, calling out and moaning together.

In the real world, though, they said nothing, neither of them moved, and that made her even more excited, because she too was free to think what she liked. She was asking him to touch her gently, she was opening her legs, she was masturbating in front of him, saying the most romantic things and the lewdest things, as if they were one and the same; she had several orgasms, waking the neighbours, waking the whole world with her cries. Here was her man, who was giving her pleasure and joy, with whom she could be the person she really was, with whom she could talk about her sexual problems, and tell him how much she would like to stay with him for the rest of the night, for the rest of the week, for the rest of her life.

Beads of sweat began to appear on their foreheads. It was the heat from the fire, one said mentally to the other. But both the man and the woman in that room had reached their limit, exhausted their imagination, experienced together an eternity of good moments. They needed to stop, because if they took one more step, the magic would be undone by reality.

Very slowly, because endings are always more difficult than beginnings, she put on her bra and hid her breasts. The universe returned to its normal place, the things around them re-emerged, she pulled up the dress that had fallen about her waist, smiled and very gently touched his face. He took her hand and pressed it to his cheek, not knowing for how long he should hold it there, or how tightly.

She wanted to tell him that she loved him. But that would spoil everything, it might frighten him or, worse, might make him say that he loved her too. Maria didn't want that: the freedom of her love depended on asking nothing and expecting nothing.

"Anyone capable of feeling knows that it is possible to experience pleasure before even touching the other person. The words, the looks, all contain the secret of the dance. But the train has arrived, we each go our separate ways. I hope to be able to join you on this journey to ... where?'

'Back to Geneva,' replied Ralf.

'Anyone who is observant, who discovers the person they have always dreamed of, knows that sexual energy comes into play before sex even takes place. The greatest pleasure isn't sex, but the passion with which it is practised. When the passion is intense, then sex joins in to complete the dance, but it is never the principal aim.'

'You're talking about love like a teacher.'

Maria went on talking, because this was her defence, her way of saying everything without committing herself to anything.

'Anyone who is in love is making love the whole time, even when they're not. When two bodies meet, it is just the cup overflowing. They can stay together for hours, even days. They begin the dance one day and finish it the next, or – such is the pleasure they experience – they may never finish it. No eleven minutes for them.'

'What?'

'I love you.'

'I love you too.'

'I'm sorry, I don't know what I'm saying.'

'Nor do I.'

She got up, kissed him and left. This time she opened the front door herself, since, according to the Brazilian superstition, the owner of the house only has to open the door on the first occasion that a guest leaves.

From Maria's diary, written the next morning:

Last night, when Ralf Hart looked at me, he opened a door, as if he were a thief; but when he left, he took nothing from me, on the contrary, he left behind him the scent of roses – he wasn't a thief, he was a bridegroom visiting me.

Every human being experiences his or her own desire; it is part of our personal treasure and, although, as an emotion, it can drive people away, generally speaking, it brings those who are important to us closer. It is an emotion chosen by my soul, and it is so intense that it can infect everything and everyone around me.

Each day I choose the truth by which I try to live. I try to be practical, efficient, professional. But I would like to be able always to choose desire as my companion. Not out of obligation, not to lessen my loneliness, but because it is good. Yes, very good.

On average, thirty-eight women worked at the Copacabana on a regular basis, but only one of them, the Filipino, Nyah, was what Maria would consider a friend. Women stayed there an average of six months minimum and three years maximum, because they would either get a proposal of marriage, be set up as a mistress, or no longer pull in the clients, in which case, Milan would delicately ask them to find somewhere else to work.

That is why it was important to respect each other's clientele and never try to seduce men who always headed for a particular girl as soon as they came in. Apart from being dishonest, it could also be very dangerous. The previous week, a Colombian woman had quietly taken a cut-throat razor out of her pocket, placed it on the glass being used by one of the Yugoslav girls, and said, in the calmest of voices, that she would mark her face if she persisted in giving in to the advances of a certain bank manager who was a regular customer. The Yugoslav said that the man was a free agent and that, if he chose her, she couldn't really say no.

That night, the man came in, greeted the Colombian woman, but went over to the Yugoslav's table. They had a drink, danced and the Yugoslav winked at the Colombian (a provocation too far in Maria's view), as if saying: 'See? He chose me!'

But that wink contained many unspoken things: he chose me because I'm prettier, because I went with him last week and he enjoyed it, because I'm young. The Colombian said nothing. When the Yugoslav came back, two hours later, the Colombian sat down beside her, took the razor out of her pocket and made a cut on the Yugoslav's face, near her ear. It wasn't a deep cut, and it wasn't dangerous, but it was enough to leave a small scar to remind her of that night. The two started fighting, blood spurted everywhere and the frightened customers fled.

When the police arrived, wanting to know what was going on, the Yugoslav said that she had cut her face on a glass that had fallen from a shelf (there are no shelves in the Copacabana). This was the law of silence, or what Italian prostitutes like to call *omertà*: any problem to be resolved in Rue de Berne, from love to death, would be resolved, but without the interference of the law. They made their own laws there.

The police knew about the *omertà* and could see that the woman was lying, but they didn't insist – arresting someone, trying them and then keeping them in prison would cost the Swiss taxpayer far too much money. Milan thanked the police for their prompt response, but, he said, it was all a misunderstanding or else a rival nightclub owner trying to make trouble.

As soon as they left, he asked the two women not to come back to his club. After all, the Copacabana was a family place (a statement Maria found hard to grasp) and had a reputation to keep up (this left her still more intrigued). There were no fights there, because the first law was to respect another woman's client.

The second law was total discretion, 'just like a Swiss bank', he said. This was largely because, there, the women could trust the clients, who were selected much as a bank selects its clients, based on the state of their current account and on personal references. Mistakes were occasionally made; there were a few rare cases of non-payment, of girls being threatened or roughed up, but in the many years he had spent struggling to create and develop his club's reputation, Milan had become an expert at recognising who should or shouldn't be invited in. None of the women knew exactly what these criteria were, but they had often seen some well-dressed man being told that the club was full that night (even though it was empty) and that it would be full the following nights too (i.e. please don't come back). They had also seen unshaven men dressed in casual clothes being enthusiastically invited by Milan to a glass of champagne. The owner of the Copacabana did not judge by appearances, and he was always right.

It was a good working relationship, and seemed to suit all parties involved. The great majority of the clientele were married, or held important positions in some company or other. Some of the women who worked there were also married and had children and went to parents' evenings at their children's schools, but knew that they ran no risk of being exposed; if one of the other parents turned up at the Copacabana, they would be compromised too and so could say nothing: that is how *omertà* worked.

There was comradeship amongst the women, but not friendship; no one talked much about their lives. In the few conversations she had had, Maria found no bitterness, guilt or sadness amongst her colleagues, only a kind of resignation, and a strangely defiant glint in the eye, as if they were proud of the way they confronted the world, independently and confidently. After a week, any new arrival was considered a 'fellow professional' and received instructions always to help keep marriages intact (a prostitute cannot be seen as a threat to the stability of the home), never to accept invitations to meet outside working hours, to listen to confessions without offering an opinion, to moan at the moment of climax (Maria learned that everyone did this, but that they hadn't told her on her very first day because it was one of the tricks of the trade), to say hello to the police in the street, to keep her work permit up to date as well as any health checks, and, finally, not to probe too deeply into the moral or legal aspects of what she was doing; they were what they were, and that was that.

Before it got busy, Maria could always be seen with a book in her hand, and she soon became known as the intellectual of the group. At first, they wanted to know if she was reading a love story, but when they saw that the books were about dry-as-dust subjects like economics, psychology and – recently – farm management, they left her alone to continue her researches and her note-taking in peace.

Because she had a lot of regular clients and because she went to the Copacabana every night, even when it wasn't busy, Maria earned both Milan's confidence and her colleagues' envy; they said she was ambitious, arrogant and thought only about earning money – the last bit was true, but she felt like asking if they weren't all there for the very same reason.

Anyway, remarks like that never killed anyone – they were part of the life of any successful person, and it was best to get used to them, rather than let herself be diverted from her two goals: going back to Brazil on the chosen date and buying a farm.

Ralf Hart was in her thoughts from morning to night now, and for the first time she was able to feel happy with an absent love – although she slightly regretted having confessed her love, thus running the risk of losing everything. But what had she got to lose, if she was asking for nothing in exchange? She remembered how her heart had beat faster when Milan mentioned that Ralf was – or had been – a special client. What did that mean? She felt betrayed and jealous.

It was normal to feel jealous, although life had taught her that it was pointless thinking you could own another person – anyone who believes that is just deceiving themselves. Despite this, she could not stop herself having these feelings of jealousy, or of having grand intellectual thoughts about it, or even thinking it was a proof of fragility.

'The strongest love is the love that can demonstrate its fragility. Anyway, if my love is real (and not just a way of distracting myself, deceiving myself, and passing the time that never seems to pass in this city), freedom will conquer jealousy and any pain it causes me, since pain is also part of the natural process. Anyone who practises sport knows this: if you want to achieve your objectives, you have to be prepared for a daily dose of pain or discomfort. At first, it's unpleasant and demotivating, but in time you come to realise that it's part of the process of feeling good, and the moment arrives when, if you don't feel pain, you have a sense that the exercises aren't having the desired effect.'

The danger lies in focusing on that pain, giving it a particular person's name, and keeping it always present in your thoughts. Maria, thank God, had managed to free herself from that.

Even so, she sometimes found herself wondering where he was, why he didn't come and see her, if he had found that whole story about the train station and repressed desire stupid, if he had gone away forever because she had confessed her love for him.

To avoid beautiful thoughts turning into suffering, she developed a method: when something positive to do with Ralf Hart came into her head – and this could be the fire and the wine, an idea she would like to discuss with him, or simply the pleasurable longing involved in wanting to know when he would come back – Maria would stop what she was doing, smile up at the sky and give thanks for being alive and to be expecting nothing from the man she loved.

On the other hand, if her heart began to complain about his absence or about things she shouldn't have said while they were together, she would say to herself:

'Oh, so you want to think about that, do you? All right, then, you do what you like, while I get on with more important things.'

She would continue to read or, if she was out, she would focus her attention on everything around her: colours, people, sounds – especially sounds, the sound of her own footsteps, of the pages turning, of cars, of fragments of conversations, and the unfortunate thought would eventually go away. If it came back five minutes later, she would repeat the process, until those thoughts, finding themselves accepted but also gently rejected, would stay away for quite considerable periods of time.

One of these 'negative thoughts' was the possibility of never seeing him again. With a little practice and a great deal of patience, she managed to transform this into a 'positive thought': when she left, Geneva would have the face of a man with old-fashioned long hair, a child-like smile and a grave voice. If someone asked her, many years later, what the place she had known in her youth was like, she could reply:

'Very beautiful, and capable of loving and being loved.'

From Maria's diary, on a slack night at the Copacabana:

After all the time I've spent with the people who come here, I have reached the conclusion that sex has come to be used as some kind of drug: in order to escape reality, to forget about problems, to relax. And like all drugs, this is a harmful and destructive practice.

If a person wants to take drugs, in the form of sex or whatever, that's their problem; the consequences of their actions will be better or worse depending on the choices they make. But if we are talking in terms of making progress in life, we must understand that 'good enough' is very different from 'best'.

Contrary to what my clients think, sex cannot be practised at any time. We all have a clock inside us, and in order to make love, the hands on both clocks have to be pointing to the same hour at the same time. That doesn't happen every day. If you love another person, you don't depend on the sex act in order to feel good. Two people who live together and love each other need to adjust the hands of their clocks, with patience and perseverance, games and 'theatrical representations', until they realise that making love is more than just an encounter, it is a genital 'embrace'.

Everything is important. If you live your life intensely, you experience pleasure all the time and don't feel the need for sex. When you have sex, it's out of a sense of abundance, because the glass of wine is so full that it overflows naturally, because it is inevitable, because you are responding to the call of life, because at that moment, and only at that moment, you have allowed yourself to lose control.

P.S. I have just re-read what I wrote. Good grief! I'm getting way too intellectual!

Shortly after writing this, and when she was preparing for another night as Understanding Mother or Innocent Girl, the door of the Copacabana opened and in walked Terence, the record company executive, one of the special clients.

Behind the bar, Milan seemed pleased: Maria had not disappointed him. Maria remembered the words that simultaneously said so much and so little: 'pain, suffering, and a great deal of pleasure'.

'I flew in from London especially to see you. I've been thinking about you a lot.'

She smiled, trying not to look too encouraging. Again he had failed to follow the ritual and hadn't asked if she wanted a drink, but just sat down at her table.

'When a teacher helps someone to discover something, the teacher always learns something new too.'

'I know what you mean,' said Maria, thinking of Ralf Hart and feeling irritated with herself for doing so. She was with another client, and she must respect him and do what she could to please him.

'Do you want to go ahead?'

A thousand francs. A hidden universe. Her boss watching her. The certainty that she could stop whenever she chose. The date set for her return to Brazil. The other man, who never came to see her.

'Are you in a hurry?' Maria asked.

He said no. What was it she wanted?

'I'd like my usual drink and my usual dance, and some respect for my profession.'

He hesitated for a moment, but it was all part of the theatre, dominating and being dominated. He bought her a drink and danced with her, then ordered a taxi and gave her the money while they drove across the city to the same hotel. They went in, he greeted the Italian porter just as he had on the night they first met, and they went up to the same suite with a view over the river.

Terence got up and took out his lighter, and only then did Maria notice that there were dozens of candles arranged around the room. He started lighting them.

'What would you like to know? Why I'm like this? Because, unless I'm very much mistaken, you really enjoyed the other evening we spent together. Do you want to know why you're like this too?'

'I was just thinking that in Brazil we have a superstition that you should never light more than three things with the same match. You're not respecting that superstition.'

He ignored her remark.

'You're like me. You're not here for the thousand francs, but out of a sense of guilt and dependency, because of your various complexes and insecurities. That is neither good nor bad, it's simply human nature.'

He picked up the remote control and changed channels several times until he found the TV news and a report on refugees trying to escape a war.

'Do you see that? Have you ever seen those programmes in which people discuss their personal problems in front of everyone? Have you been to a newspaper kiosk and seen the headlines? The world enjoys suffering and pain. There's sadism in the way we look at these things, and masochism in our conclusion that we don't need to know all this in order to be happy, and yet we watch other people's tragedies and sometimes suffer along with them.'

He poured out two glasses of champagne, turned off the television and continued lighting candles, in contravention of the superstition Maria had mentioned.

'As I say, it's the human condition. Ever since we were expelled from paradise, we have either been suffering, making other people suffer or watching the suffering of others. It's beyond our control.'

From outside came the sound of thunder and lightning; a huge storm was approaching.

'But I can't do it,' Maria said. 'It seems ridiculous to me pretending that you're my master and I'm your slave. We don't need "theatre" to find suffering; life offers us more than enough opportunities.'

Terence had just finished lighting the candles. He picked one up and placed it in the middle of the table, then served more champagne, and caviar. Maria was drinking quickly, thinking about the one thousand francs in her bag, about this stranger who both fascinated and frightened her, and about how she could control her fear. She knew that, with this man, no night would ever be the same as another; she could not intimidate him in any way.

'Sit down.'

His voice alternated between being gentle and authoritarian. Maria obeyed, and a wave of heat swept up her body; that order was familiar, she felt more secure.

'It's theatre. I've got to get involved in the play.'

It was nice being ordered around. She didn't have to think, just obey. She asked for more champagne, and he brought vodka; it went to one's head more quickly, loosened one up, and went better with the caviar.

He opened the bottle; Maria was more or less drinking alone, while she listened to the thunder and lightning outside. Everything was conspiring to make the moment perfect, as if the energies of the skies and the earth were also showing their violent side.

After a while, Terence took a small suitcase out of the wardrobe and placed it on the bed.

'Don't move.'

Maria sat motionless. He opened the suitcase and took out two pairs of chrome metal handcuffs.

'Sit with your legs apart.'

She obeyed – impotent out of choice, submissive because she wanted to be. She saw him looking between her legs, he could see her black pants, her long stockings, her thighs, he could imagine her pubic hair, her sex.

'Stand up!'

She leaped up from her chair. She found it hard to stand straight and realised that she was drunker than she thought.

'Don't look at me. Lower your head, respect your master!'

Before she could lower her head, she saw a slender whip being removed from the suitcase, then cracking through the air, as if it had a life of its own.

'Drink. Keep your head down, but drink.'

She drank another one, two, three glasses of vodka. This wasn't just theatre now, it was reality: control was out of her hands. She felt like an object, a mere instrument, and incredible though it may seem, that feeling of submission gave her a sense of complete freedom. She was no longer the teacher, the one who instructs, consoles, listens to confessions, the one who excites; before the awesome power of this man, she was just a girl from the interior of Brazil.

'Take off your clothes.'

The order was delivered abruptly, without a flicker of desire, and yet, nothing could have been more erotic. Keeping her head down as a sign of reverence, Maria unbuttoned her dress and let it slip to the floor.

'You're not behaving yourself, you know.'

Again the whip cracked through the air.

'You need to be punished. How dare a girl your age contradict me? You should be on your knees before me!'

Maria made as if to kneel down, but the whip brought her up short; for the first time it touched her flesh – her buttocks. It stung, but seemed to leave no mark.

'Did I tell you to kneel down?'

'No.'

The whip again flicked across her buttocks.

'Say, "No, sir!"'

Another stinging whiplash. For a fraction of a second, it occurred to her that she could either stop this right now or else choose to go through with it, not for the money, but because of what he had said the first time – that you only know yourself when you go beyond your limits.

And this was new, it was an Adventure, and she could decide later on if she wanted to continue, but at that moment, she had ceased to be the girl with just three aims in life, who earned her living with her body, who had met a man who had an open fire and interesting stories to tell. Here, she was no one, and being no one meant that she could be everything she had ever dreamed of.

'Take the rest of your clothes off. And walk up and down so that I can see you.'

Once more she obeyed, keeping her head down, saying not a word. The man who was watching her, still fully dressed and utterly impassive, was not the same person who had chatted to her on their way here from the club – he was a Ulysses who had travelled from London, a Theseus come down from the heavens, a kidnapper invading the safest city in the world, and who had the coldest heart on earth. She removed her pants and her bra, feeling at once defenceless and protected. The whip cracked again, this time without touching her body.

'Keep your head down! You're here to be humiliated, to submit to my every desire, do you understand?'

'Yes, sir.'

He grabbed her arms and put the first pair of handcuffs on her wrists.

'You're going to get a good beating. Until you learn to behave yourself.'

He slapped her bottom with the flat of his hand. Maria cried out; this time it had hurt.

'Oh, so you're complaining, are you? Well, I haven't even started yet.'

Before she could do anything, he had placed a leather gag on her mouth. It didn't stop her speaking, she could still say 'yellow' or 'red', but she felt now that it was her destiny to allow this man to do whatever he wished with her, and there was no way she could escape now. She was naked, gagged and handcuffed, with vodka flowing in her veins rather than blood.

Another slap on her buttocks.

'Walk up and down!'

Maria started to walk, obeying his commands: 'stop', 'turn to the right', 'sit down', 'open your legs'. He slapped her again and again, whether she deserved it or not, and she felt the pain and felt the humiliation – which was more intense and more potent than the pain – and she felt as if she were in another world, in which nothing existed, and it was an almost religious feeling: self-annihilation, subjection, and a complete loss of any sense of Ego, desire or self-will. She was very wet and very aroused, but unable to understand what was going on.

'Down on your knees again!'

Since she always kept her head down, as a sign of obedience and humiliation, Maria could not see exactly what was happening, but she noticed that in that other universe, on that other planet, the man was breathing hard, worn out with wielding the whip and spanking her hard on the buttocks, whilst she felt herself filling up with strength and energy. She had lost all shame now, and wasn't bothered about showing her pleasure; she started to moan, pleading with him to touch her, but, instead, the man grabbed her and threw her onto the bed.

He violently forced her legs apart – although she knew this violence would not actually harm her – and tied each leg to one corner of the bed. Now that her wrists were handcuffed behind her, her legs splayed, her mouth gagged, when would he penetrate her? Couldn't he see that she was ready, that she wanted to serve him, that she was his slave, his creature, his object, and would do anything he ordered her to do?

'Would you like me to take you further still?'

She saw him place the end of the whip handle against her vagina. He rubbed it up and down, and when it touched her clitoris, she lost all control. She had no idea how long they had been there nor how many times she had been spanked, but suddenly she came and had the orgasm which, in all those months, dozens, no, hundreds of men had failed to give her. There was a burst of light, she felt herself entering a kind of black hole in her soul, in which intense pain and fear mingled with total pleasure, pushing her beyond all previously known limits and she moaned and screamed, her voice muffled by the gag, she writhed about on the bed, feeling the handcuffs cutting into her wrists and the leather thongs bruising her ankles, she moved as never before precisely because she could not move, she screamed as never before because she had a gag on her mouth and no one would be able to hear her. This was pain and pleasure, the end of the whip handle pressing ever harder against her clitoris and the orgasm flooding out of her mouth, her vagina, her pores, her eyes, her skin.

She entered a kind of trance, and slowly, very slowly, she began to come down; there was no whip pressing between her legs now, just sweat-drenched hair, kind hands removing the handcuffs, untying the leather thongs around her ankles.

She lay there, confused, unable to look at the man because she was ashamed of herself, of her screams, of her orgasm. He was stroking her hair and he too was breathing hard, but the pleasure had been entirely hers; he had not enjoyed a single moment of ecstasy.

Her naked body embraced that of this fully clothed man, who was exhausted from shouting orders and keeping tight control of the situation. She didn't know what to say, how to continue, but she felt safe and protected, because he had invited her to go to a place inside herself that she had never known before; he was her protector and her master.

She started to cry, and he waited patiently until she had finished.

'What did you do to me?' she asked tearfully.

'What you wanted me to do.'

She looked at him, feeling that she needed him desperately.

'I didn't force you or oblige you to do anything, nor did I hear you say "yellow"; I had only the power you gave me. There was no obligation, no blackmail on my part, only your will; you may have been the slave and I the master, but my only power was to push you in the direction of your own freedom.'

Handcuffs. Leather thongs around her ankles. A gag. Humiliation that was more intense and more potent than any pain. And yet – he was quite right – the feeling was one of total freedom. Maria felt full of energy and vigour and was surprised to see that the man beside her was utterly exhausted.

'Did you come?'

'No,' he said. 'The master is here to drive the slave on. The pleasure of the slave is the joy of the master.'

None of this made sense, because it wasn't the way it was in stories, it wasn't the way it was in real life. But here in this fantasy world, she was full of light, while he seemed opaque, drained.

'You can leave whenever you want,' Terence said.

'I don't want to leave, I want to understand.'

'There's nothing to understand.'

She got up in all the beauty and intensity of her nakedness and poured two glasses of wine. She lit two cigarettes and gave him one of them – the roles were reversed, she was now the mistress serving the slave, rewarding him for the pleasure he had given her.

'I'll get dressed and then I'll leave, but, first, I'd like to talk a little.'

'There's nothing to talk about. That's all I wanted, and you were marvellous. I'm tired now and I have to go back to London tomorrow.'

He lay down and closed his eyes. Maria didn't know if he was just pretending to sleep and she didn't care; she smoked a leisurely cigarette and slowly sipped her wine, with her face pressed against the window pane, looking out at the lake opposite and wishing that someone, on the other shore, could see her like this – naked, replete, satisfied, confident.

She got dressed and left without saying goodbye, and was not bothered whether she opened the door or he did, because she wasn't sure that she wanted to come back.

Terence heard the door close, waited to see if she would come back, saying that she had forgotten something, and only after a few minutes did he get up and light another cigarette.

The girl had style, he thought. She had withstood the whip well, although this was the oldest, the most common and the least severe of the punishments. For a moment, he sat remembering the first time he had experienced that mysterious relationship between two beings who want to be close, but can only be so by inflicting suffering.

Millions of couples out there practised the art of sadomasochism every day, without even realising it. They went to work, came back, complained about everything, insulted their wife or were insulted by her, felt wretched, but were, nonetheless, tightly bound to their own unhappiness, not realising that all it would take was a single gesture, a final goodbye, to free them from that oppression. Terence had experienced this with his wife, a well-known English singer; he was tormented by jealousy, he made scenes, and spent whole days dosed up with painkillers, whole nights hopelessly drunk. She loved him and couldn't understand why he behaved like that; he loved her and couldn't understand his own behaviour. It was as if the agony that the one inflicted on the other was necessary, fundamental to life.

One day, a musician – whom he had always thought of as very strange, because he seemed so normal in the midst of all those exotic people – left a book behind in the studio: *Venus in Furs* by Leopold von Sacher-Masoch. Terence started leafing through it and, as he read, he began to understand himself better.

'The lovely woman took off her clothes and picked up a long, short-handled whip. "You asked for it," she said, "so I'm going to whip you." "Oh, yes," murmured her lover, "please, I beg you."'

His wife was on the other side of the glass screen, rehearsing. She had asked them to turn off the microphones that allowed the technicians to listen in to everything, and they had done so. Terence was thinking that perhaps she was making a date with the pianist, and he realised that she was driving him mad, but it was as if he was so accustomed to suffering now that he could not live without it.

'I'm going to whip you,' said the naked woman in the book he was reading. 'Oh, yes, please, I beg you.'

He was a good-looking man, and a force to be reckoned with in the record company, why did he need to lead such a life?

Because he wanted to. He deserved to suffer because life had been so good to him, and he wasn't worthy of all these blessings – money, respect, fame. He felt that his career was leading him to a point where he would become dependent on success, and that frightened him, because he had seen a lot of people plummet from the heights.

He read the book. He started reading everything he could find about the mysterious union between pain and pleasure. His wife found the videos he was renting and the books he was hiding from her, and asked him what it was all about, was he sick? Terence said no, it was just research he was doing for a new cover. Then he said nonchalantly:

'Perhaps we should try it.'

They did. They began very timidly, using the manuals they found in porn shops. Gradually, they developed new techniques, took their activities to dangerous limits, and yet they felt that their marriage was even stronger. They were accomplices in something hidden, forbidden, proscribed.

Their joint experience was transformed into art: they created new outfits – leather with metal studs. His wife went on stage wearing boots and a suspender belt and wielding a whip, and the audience went wild. Her new record shot to the top of the charts in England and went on to triumph in the rest of Europe. Terence was surprised how young people accepted his personal fantasies as perfectly natural, and the only explanation he could find was that it provided a means of expressing repressed violence in an intense but inoffensive manner.

The whip came to be the group's logo and was reproduced on T-shirts, fake tattoos, stickers and postcards. Terence's intellectual bent drove him to track down the origins of all this, so that he could understand himself better.

These origins did not lie, as he had told Maria, with those penitents trying to drive away the Black Death. Ever since the Dark Ages, man has understood that suffering, if confronted without fear, is his passport to freedom.

Egypt, Rome and Persia all shared the notion that a man can save his country and his world by sacrificing himself. Whenever there was a great natural disaster in China, the emperor was punished, because he was the divinity's Earthly representative. In ancient Greece, the finest Spartan warriors were whipped once a year, from morning till night, in homage to the goddess Artemis, while the crowd urged them on, calling on them to withstand the pain with dignity, for it was preparing them for the world of war. At the end of the day, the priests would examine the wounds on the warriors' backs and use them to predict the city's future.

The priests of the desert, in an ancient, fourth-century Christian community that grew up around a monastery in Alexandria, used flagellation as a way of driving out demons or of proving the futility of the body in the spiritual search. The history of saints was full of similar examples – St Rosa running through the garden, letting the thorns tear her skin, St Domingos Loricatus whipping himself every night before sleeping, the martyrs who voluntarily offered themselves up to a slow death on the cross or being torn apart by wild animals. They all said that pain, once mastered, could lead to religious ecstasy.

Recent, unconfirmed studies indicated that a particular kind of fungus with hallucinogenic properties grew in the wounds and caused visions. The pleasure was so intense that the practice soon left the monasteries and convents and spread throughout the world.

In 1718, *A Treatise on Self-flagellation* was published, which showed how to achieve pleasure through pain, but without harming the body. At the end of that century, there were dozens of places in Europe where people were prepared to suffer in order to attain joy. There are records of kings and princesses who had their slaves whip them, until they found that another kind of pleasure – albeit more exhausting and less gratifying – was to be found not only in being whipped, but also in inflicting pain.

While he was smoking his cigarette, Terence took a certain pleasurable pride in knowing that most people would be unable to understand what he was thinking.

It was better to belong to an exclusive club to which only the chosen had access. He remembered again how the torment of marriage had been transformed into the miracle of marriage. His wife knew that he visited Geneva for this purpose and she didn't mind; on the contrary, in this sick world, she was glad that her husband got the reward he wanted after a hard week at work.

The girl who had just left the room had understood everything. He felt that his soul was very close to hers, although he wasn't yet ready to fall in love, for he loved his wife. But he liked to think that he was free and could dream of a new relationship.

All he had to do was to get her to attempt the next and most difficult stage: the transformation into Sacher-Masoch's 'Venus in Furs', the Dominatrix, the Mistress, capable of humiliating and punishing without pity. If she passed the test, he was ready to open his heart and let her in.

From Maria's diary, when she was still drunk on vodka and pleasure:

> *When I had nothing to lose, I had everything. When I stopped being who I am, I found myself.*
>
> *When I experienced humiliation and total submission, I was free. I don't know if I'm ill, if it was all a dream, or if it only happens once. I know that I can*

perfectly well live without it, but I would like to do it again, to repeat the experience, to go still further.

I was a bit frightened by the pain, but it wasn't as bad as the humiliation, and it was just a pretext. When I had my first orgasm in many months, despite all the many men I've been with and the many different things they've done with my body, I felt – is this possible? – closer to God. I remembered what he said about how the flagellants, in offering up their pain for the salvation of humanity, found pleasure. I didn't want to save humanity, or him or me; I was just there.

The art of sex is the art of controlled abandon.

It wasn't theatre this time, they were in a real train station, at Maria's request, because she liked the pizza you could buy there. There was nothing wrong with being a bit wayward sometimes. Ralf ought to have come to see her the day before, when she was still a woman in search of love, an open fire, wine and desire. But life had chosen otherwise, and today she had got through the whole day without once having to make herself concentrate on the sounds around her or on the present moment, simply because she hadn't thought about Ralf; she had discovered other more interesting things to think about.

What was she to do with this man beside her, who was eating a pizza he probably didn't like and who was just passing the time until the moment came for them to go to his house? When he had come into the club and offered her a drink, she had thought of telling him that she wasn't interested any more and that he should find someone else; on the other hand, she had an enormous need to talk to someone about the previous night.

She had tried talking to one or two of the other prostitutes who served the 'special clients', but none of them would tell her anything, because Maria was bright, she learned quickly and had become the great threat in the Copacabana. Of all the men she knew, Ralf Hart was the only one who would understand, because Milan considered him too to be a 'special client'. But he looked at her with eyes alight with

193

love, and that made things difficult; it was best to say nothing.

'What do you know about pain, suffering and pleasure?'

She had once again failed to keep her thoughts to herself.

Ralf stopped eating his pizza.

'Everything. And it doesn't interest me in the least.'

The reply had been instant, and Maria was shocked. Was she the only person in the world who didn't know everything? What kind of world was this?

'I've confronted my demons and my dark side,' Ralf went on. 'I've been to the very depths and tried everything, not just in that area, but in many others too. On the last night we met, however, I went beyond my limits through desire, not pain. I plunged into the depths of my soul and I know that I still want good things, many good things from this life.'

He wanted to say: 'One of those good things is you, so, please, don't go down that path.' But he didn't have the courage; instead, he called a taxi and asked the driver to take them to the lake shore, where, an eternity before, they had walked together on the day they first met. Maria understood the request and said nothing; her instinct told her that she had a lot to lose, although her mind was still drunk on what had happened the night before.

She only awoke from her passive state when they reached the gardens beside the lake; although it was still summer, it was already starting to get very cold at night.

'What are we doing here?' she asked, as they got out of the taxi. 'It's windy. I might catch a cold.'

'I've been thinking about what you said at the train station, about suffering and pleasure. Take your shoes off.'

She remembered that once, one of her clients had asked the same thing, and had been aroused simply by looking at her feet. Would Adventure never leave her in peace?

'I'll catch a cold.'

'Do as I say,' he insisted. 'You won't catch a cold if we're quick. Believe in me, as I believe in you.'

For some reason, Maria realised that he was trying to help her; perhaps because he himself had once drunk of some very bitter water and was afraid that she was running the same risk. She didn't want to be helped; she was happy with her new world, in which she was learning that suffering wasn't a problem any more. Then she thought of Brazil, of the impossibility of finding a partner with whom to share that different universe, and since Brazil was the most important thing in her life, she took off her shoes. The ground was covered in small stones that immediately tore her stockings, but that didn't matter, she could buy some more.

'Take off your jacket.'

She could have said 'no', but, since last night, she had got used to the joy of saying 'yes' to everything that came her way. She took off her jacket, and her body, still warm, took a while to react, then gradually the cold began to get to her.

'We can talk and walk at the same time.'

'I can't walk here, the ground's covered in stones.'

'Exactly. I want you to feel these stones, I want them to hurt you and bruise you, because, just as I did, you have started to associate suffering with pleasure, and I need to tear that out of your soul.'

Maria felt like saying: 'There's no need, I like it.' Instead, she began walking slowly along, and the soles of her feet began to burn with the cold and the sharp edges of the stones.

'One of my exhibitions took me to Japan, just when I was immersed in what you called "pain, suffering and pleasure". At the time, I thought there was no way back, that I would go deeper and deeper down, until there was nothing left in my life but the desire to punish and be punished.

'After all, we are human beings, we are born full of guilt; we feel terrified when happiness becomes a real possibility; and we die wanting to punish everyone else because we feel impotent, ill-used and unhappy. To pay for one's sins and be able to punish the sinners, wouldn't that be delicious? Oh, yes, wonderful.'

Maria was still walking, the pain and the cold were making it hard for her to concentrate on what he was saying, but she was doing her best.

'I noticed the marks on your wrists today.'

The handcuffs. She had put on several bracelets to disguise the marks, but the expert eye knows what to look for.

'Now, if your recent experiences are leading you to take that step, I won't stop you, but you should know that none of it has anything to do with real life.'

'Take what step?'

'Into pain and pleasure, sadism and masochism. Call it what you like, but if you're sure that's the right path for you, I will be sad, I'll remember that feeling of desire, our meetings, our walk along the road to Santiago, your light. I will treasure the pen you gave me, and every time I light the fire, I will remember you. But I will never again come looking for you.'

Maria felt afraid; she felt it was time to recant, to tell him the truth, to stop pretending that she knew more than he did.

'What I experienced recently – last night, in fact – was something I've never experienced before. And it frightens me to think that I could only find myself at the very limits of degradation.'

It was becoming difficult to speak – her teeth were chattering and her feet were really hurting.

'My exhibition was held in a region called Kumano, and one of the people who came to see it was a woodcutter,' Ralf went on, as if he hadn't heard what she had said. 'He didn't like my pictures, but he was able to see, through the paintings, what I was experiencing and feeling. The following day, he came to my hotel and asked me if I was happy; if I was, I should continue doing what I liked. If I wasn't, I should go and spend a few days with him.

'He made me walk on stones, just as I am making you do today. He made me feel the cold. He forced me to understand the beauty of pain, except that the pain was imposed by nature, not by man. He called this *shu-gen-do*, a very ancient practice apparently.

'He told me that I was someone who wasn't afraid of pain, and that was good, because in order to master the soul, one must also learn to master the body. He told me, too, that I was using pain in the wrong way, and that was very bad.

'This uneducated woodcutter thought he knew me better than I did myself, and that annoyed me, but at the same time, I felt proud to think that my paintings were capable of expressing exactly what I was feeling.'

Maria was aware of a sharp stone cutting into her foot, but she could barely feel it for the cold, her body was growing numb, and she could only just follow what Ralf Hart was saying. Why was it that in God's holy world men were only interested in showing her pain. Sacred pain, pain with pleasure, pain with explanations or without, but always pain, pain, pain ...

Her cut foot stumbled on another stone; she smothered a cry and continued on. At first, she had managed to maintain her integrity, her self-control, what he called her 'light'. Now, though, she was walking very slowly, with both her stomach and her mind churning: she felt as if she were about to throw up. She considered stopping, because none of this made any sense, but she didn't.

And she didn't stop out of respect for herself; she could stand that barefoot walk as long as she had to, because it wouldn't last all her life. And suddenly another thought crossed her mind: what if she couldn't go to the Copacabana tomorrow night because she had injured her feet, or because of a fever brought on by the flu that would doubtless install itself in her overexposed body? She thought of the customers who would be expecting her, of Milan who so trusted her, of the money she wouldn't earn, of the farm, of her proud parents. But the suffering soon drove out all such thoughts, and she kept placing one foot in front of the other, longing for Ralf Hart to recognise the effort she was making and to tell her she could stop and put her shoes back on again.

He seemed entirely indifferent, distant, as if this were the only way of freeing her from something she didn't as yet really know about, something she found very seductive, but which would leave far deeper marks than any handcuffs. Although she knew he was trying to help her, and however hard she tried to go forward and show him the light of her willpower, the pain would not allow her any thoughts, noble or profane; it was just pain, filling everything, frightening her and forcing her to think that she did have limits and that she wasn't going to make it.

But she took one step.

And another.

The pain seemed about to invade her soul now and undermine her spiritually, because it's one thing to put on a bit of theatre in a five-star hotel, naked, with vodka and caviar inside you and a whip between your legs, but it's quite another to be cold and barefoot, with stones lacerating your feet. She was disoriented, she couldn't think of a single thing to say to Ralf Hart; all that existed in her universe were those small, sharp stones that formed the path between the trees.

Then, just when she thought she was about to give up, she was filled by a strange feeling: she had reached her limit, and beyond it was an empty space, in which she seemed to float above herself, unaware of what she was feeling. Was this what the penitents had experienced? At the far extremity of pain, she had discovered a door into a different level of consciousness, and there was no room now for anything but implacable nature and her own invincible self.

Everything around her became a dream: the ill-lit garden, the dark lake, the man walking beside her, saying nothing, the occasional couple out for a stroll, who failed to notice that she was barefoot and having difficulty walking. She didn't know if it was the cold or the pain, but she suddenly lost all sense of her own body and entered a state in which there was no desire and no fear, only a mysterious – how could she describe it? – a mysterious peace. The pain barrier was not a barrier for her; she could go beyond it.

She thought of all the people enduring unasked-for suffering and there she was, bringing suffering upon herself, but that didn't matter any more, she had crossed the frontiers of the body, and now there was only soul, 'light', a kind of void, which someone, some day, called Paradise. There are certain sufferings which can only be forgotten once we have succeeded in floating above our own pain.

The next thing she knew, Ralf was picking her up and putting his jacket around her shoulders. She must have fainted from the cold, but she didn't care; she was happy, she hadn't been afraid – she had come through. She had not humbled herself before him.

The minutes became hours, she must have gone to sleep in his arms, because when she woke up, although it was still dark, she was in a room with a TV in one corner, and nothing else. White, empty.

Ralf appeared with a cup of hot chocolate.

'Good,' he said. 'You got to the place you needed to get to.'

'I don't want hot chocolate, I want wine. And I want to go downstairs to our place by the fire, with books all around us.'

She had said 'our place'. That wasn't what she had planned.

She looked at her feet; apart from a small cut, there were just a few red marks, which would disappear in a few hours' time. With some difficulty, she went downstairs, without really looking around her. She went and sat down on the rug by the fire – she had discovered that she always felt good there, as if that really was her 'place' in the house.

'The woodcutter told me that whenever you do some form of physical exercise, when you demand the maximum from your body, the mind gains a strange spiritual strength, which has to do with the "light" I saw in you. What did you feel?'

'I felt that pain is woman's friend.'

'That is the danger.'

'I also felt that pain has its limits.'

'That is the salvation. Don't forget that.'

Maria's mind was still confused; she had experienced that 'peace' when she had gone beyond her own limits. He had shown her a different kind of suffering that had also given her a strange pleasure.

Ralf picked up a large file and opened it up in front of her. It contained drawings.

'The history of prostitution. That's what you asked me for when we met.'

Yes, she had, but it had only been a way of making conversation, of trying to appear interesting. It was of no importance now.

'All this time, I've been sailing in uncharted waters. I didn't think there was a history, I thought it was just the oldest profession in the world, as people say. But there is a history, or, rather, two histories.'

'And what are these drawings?'

Ralf Hart looked slightly disappointed at her apparent lack of interest in what he had said, but quickly set aside these feelings and went on.

'They're the things I jotted down as I was reading, researching, learning.'

'Let's talk about that another day. I don't want to change the subject today. I need to understand about pain.'

'You experienced pain yesterday and you discovered that it led to pleasure. You experienced it today and found peace. That's why I'm telling you: don't get used to it, because it's very easy to become habituated; it's a very powerful drug. It's in our daily lives, in our hidden suffering, in the sacrifices we make, blaming love for the destruction of our dreams. Pain is frightening when it shows its real face, but it's seductive when it comes disguised as sacrifice or self-denial. Or cowardice. However much we may reject it, we human beings always find a way of being with pain, of flirting with it and making it part of our lives.'

'I don't believe that. No one wants to suffer.'

'If you think you can live without suffering, that's a great step forward, but don't imagine that other people will understand you. True, no one wants to suffer, and yet nearly everyone seeks out pain and sacrifice, and then they feel justified, pure, deserving of the respect of their children, husbands, neighbours, God. Don't let's think about that now; all you need to know is that what makes the world go round is not the search for pleasure, but the renunciation of all that is important.

'Does a soldier go to war in order to kill the enemy? No, he goes in order to die for his country. Does a wife want to show her husband how happy she is? No, she wants him to see how devoted she is, how she suffers in order to make him happy. Does the husband go to work thinking he will find personal fulfilment there? No, he is giving his sweat and tears for the good of the family. And so it goes on: sons give up their dreams to please their parents, parents give up their lives in order to please their children; pain and suffering are used to justify the one thing that should bring only joy: love.'

'Stop.'

Ralf stopped. It was the right moment to change the subject, and he started showing her drawing after drawing. At first, it all seemed rather confusing: there were a few outlines of people, but also scrawls and scribbles, geometric shapes and colours. Gradually, though, she began to understand what he was saying, because each word he spoke was accompanied by a gesture of the hand, and each phrase placed her in the world which, up until then, she had always denied she was part of – telling herself that it was just one stage in her life, a way of earning money, nothing more.

'Yes, I discovered that there is not just one history of prostitution, but two. The first one you know all too well, because it is your history too: a pretty young girl, for reasons which she has chosen or which have chosen her, decides that the only way she can survive is by selling her body. Some end up ruling nations, as Messalina did in Rome, others become legendary figures, like Madame du Barry, still others chase after adventure and misfortune, like the spy, Mata Hari. But the majority never have their moment of glory, are never faced by a great challenge: they will always be young girls from the interior in search of fame, a husband, adventure, but who end up discovering quite a different reality, into which they plunge for a time, and to which they become accustomed, always believing that they are in control and yet ultimately unable to do anything else.

'Artists have been making sculptures and paintings and writing books for more than three thousand years. In just the same way, throughout all that time, prostitutes have carried on their work as if nothing very much ever changes. Would you like to know details?'

Maria nodded. She needed time in order to understand about pain, although she was starting to feel as if something very bad had left her body during that walk in the park.

'Prostitutes appear in classical texts, in Egyptian hieroglyphs, in Sumerian writings, in the Old and New Testament.

But the profession only started to become organised in the sixth century BC, when a Greek legislator, Solon, set up state-controlled brothels and began imposing taxes on "the skin trade". Athenian businessmen were pleased because what was once prohibited became legal. The prostitutes, on the other hand, started to be classified according to how much tax they paid.

'The cheapest were the *pornai*, slaves who belonged to the owners of the establishment. Next came the *peripatetica*, who picked up her clients in the street. Lastly, the most expensive and highest quality, was the *hetaera*, the female companion, who accompanied businessmen on their trips, dined in chic restaurants, controlled her own money, gave advice and meddled in the political life of the city. As you see, what happened then still happens now.

'In the Middle Ages, because of sexually transmitted diseases ...'

Silence, fear of catching a cold, the heat of the fire – necessary now to warm her body and her soul ... Maria didn't want to hear any more history, it gave her a sense that the world had stopped, that everything was being endlessly repeated, and that mankind would never give sex the respect it deserved.

'You don't seem very interested.'

She pulled herself together. After all, he was the man to whom she had decided to give her heart, although now she wasn't so sure.

'I'm not interested in what I know about; it just makes me sad. You said there was another history.'

'The other history is exactly the opposite: sacred prostitution.'

She had suddenly emerged from her somnolent state and was listening to him intently. Sacred prostitution? Earning money from sex and yet still able to approach God?

'The Greek historian, Herodotus, wrote of Babylonia: "They have a strange custom here, by which every woman born in Sumeria is obliged, at least once in her lifetime, to go to the temple of the goddess Ishtar and give her body to a stranger, as a symbol of hospitality and for a symbolic price."'

She would ask him about that goddess later; perhaps she would help her to recover something she had lost, although just what that was she did not know.

'The influence of the goddess Ishtar spread throughout the Middle East, as far as Sardinia, Sicily and the Mediterranean ports. Later, during the Roman Empire, another goddess, Vesta, demanded total virginity or total surrender. In order to keep the sacred fire burning, the women serving her temple were responsible for initiating young men and kings on the path of sexuality – they sang erotic hymns, entered trance-like states and gave their ecstasy to the universe in a kind of communion with the divinity.'

Ralf Hart showed her a photocopy of some ancient lyrics, with a translation in German at the foot of the page. He read slowly, translating each line as he went:

> *When I am sitting at the door of a tavern,*
> *I, Ishtar, the goddess,*
> *Am prostitute, mother, wife, divinity.*
> *I am what people call life,*
> *Although you call it death.*

I am what people call Law,
Although you call it Delinquency.
I am what you seek
And what you find.
I am what you scattered
And the pieces you now gather up.'

Maria was sobbing softly, and Ralf Hart laughed; his vital energy was returning, his 'light' was beginning to shine again. It was best to continue the history, to show her the drawings, to make her feel loved.

'No one knows why sacred prostitution disappeared, since it had lasted not centuries, perhaps, but for at least two millennia. Maybe it was disease or because society changed its rules when it changed religions. Anyway, it no longer exists, and will never exist again; nowadays, men control the world, and the term serves only to create a stigma, and any woman who steps out of line is automatically dubbed a prostitute.'

'Could you come to the Copacabana tomorrow?'

Ralf didn't understand why she was asking this, but he agreed at once.

From Maria's diary, after the night she walked barefoot in the Jardin Anglais in Geneva:

I don't care whether it was once sacred or not, I HATE WHAT I DO. It's destroying my soul, making me lose touch with myself, teaching me that pain is a reward, that money buys everything and justifies everything.

207

No one around me is happy; the clients know they are paying for something that should be free, and that's depressing. The women know that they have to sell something which they would like to give out of pleasure and affection, and that is destructive. I've struggled long and hard before writing this, before accepting how unhappy and dissatisfied I am – I needed and I still need to hold out for a few more weeks.

But I cannot simply do nothing, pretend that everything is normal, that it's just a stage, a phase of my life. I want to forget it, I need to love – that's all, I need to love.

Life is too short, or too long, for me to allow myself the luxury of living it so badly.

It isn't his house. It isn't her house. It isn't Brazil or Switzerland. It's a hotel, which could be anywhere in the world, furnished, like all hotel rooms, in a way that tries to create a familiar atmosphere, but which only makes it seem all the more impersonal.

It isn't the hotel with the lovely view of the lake and the memory of pain, suffering and ecstasy; it looks out onto the road to Santiago, a route of pilgrimage not penance, a place where people meet in the cafés along the road, discover each other's 'light', talk, become friends, fall in love. It's raining, and at this time of night, no one is walking there, although they have for years, decades, centuries – perhaps the road needs to breathe, to rest from the many steps that trudge along it every day.

Turn out the light. Close the curtains.

She asks him to take his clothes off and she does the same. Darkness is never absolute, and as soon as her eyes become accustomed to it, she can see the man's silhouette, outlined against the faintest of lights coming from who knows where. The last time they met for this purpose, she had left only part of her body naked.

She takes two carefully folded handkerchiefs, which have been washed and rinsed several times to get rid of the slightest trace of perfume or soap. She goes over to him and asks him to blindfold himself. He hesitates for a moment, and makes some remark about various hells he has been through before. She says it's nothing to do with that, she just needs total darkness; now it is her turn to teach him something, just as yesterday he taught her about pain. He gives in and puts on the blindfold. She does the same; now there is not a glimmer of light, they are in absolute darkness, and they have to hold hands in order to reach the bed.

'No, we mustn't lie down. Let's sit as we always do, face to face, only a little closer, so that my knees touch your knees.'

She has always wanted to do this, but she never had what she most needed: time. Not with her first boyfriend, or with the man who penetrated her for the first time. Not with the Arab who paid her a thousand francs, perhaps hoping for more than she was able to give him, although a thousand francs wouldn't be enough for her to buy what she wanted. Not with the many men who had passed through her body, who have come and gone between her legs, sometimes thinking about themselves, sometimes thinking about her too, sometimes harbouring romantic dreams, sometimes instinctively repeating certain words because they have been told that that is what men do, and that if they don't, they are not real men.

She thinks of her diary. She has had enough, she wants the remaining weeks to pass quickly, and that is why she is giving herself to this man, because the light of her own love lies hidden there. Original sin was not the apple that Eve ate, it was her belief that Adam needed to share precisely the thing she had tasted. Eve was afraid to follow her path without someone to help her, and so she wanted to share what she was feeling.

Certain things cannot be shared. Nor can we be afraid of the oceans into which we plunge of our own free will; fear cramps everyone's style. Man goes through hell in order to understand this. Love one another, but let's not try to possess one another.

I love this man sitting before me now, because I do not possess him and he does not possess me. We are free in our mutual surrender; I need to repeat this dozens, hundreds, millions of time, until I finally believe my own words.

She thinks about the other prostitutes who work with her. She thinks about her mother and her friends. They all believe that man feels desire for only eleven minutes a day, and that they'll pay a fortune for it. That's not true; a man is also a woman; he wants to find someone, to give meaning to his life.

Does her mother behave just as she does and pretend to have an orgasm with her father? Or in the interior of Brazil, is it still forbidden for a woman to take pleasure in sex? She knows so little of life and love, and now – with her eyes blindfolded and with all the time in the world, she is discovering the origin of everything, and everything begins where and how she would like it to have begun.

Touch. Forget prostitutes, clients, her mother and her father, now she is in total darkness. She has spent the whole afternoon wondering what she could give to a man who had restored her dignity and made her understand that the search for happiness is more important than the need for pain.

I would like to give him the happiness of teaching me something new, just as yesterday he taught me about suffering, street prostitutes and sacred prostitutes. I saw how much he enjoys teaching me things, so let him teach me, guide me. I would like to know how one reaches the body, without going via the soul, penetration, orgasm.

She holds out her hand and asks him to do the same. She whispers a few words, saying that tonight, in this no-man's-land, she would like him to discover her skin, the boundary between her and the world. She asks him to touch her, to feel her with his hands, because bodies always understand each other, even when souls do not. He begins touching her, and she touches him too, and, as if by prior agreement, they both avoid the parts of the body where sexual energy surfaces most rapidly.

His fingers touch her face, and she can smell just a hint of ink on them, a smell that will stay there forever, even if he washes his hands thousands and millions of times, a smell which was there when he was born, when he saw his first tree, his first house, and decided to draw them in his dreams. He must be able to smell something on her hands too, but she doesn't know what, and doesn't want to ask, because at that moment everything is body, and the rest is silence.

She caresses and is caressed. She could stay like this all night, because it is so pleasurable and won't necessarily end in sex, and at that moment, precisely because there is no obligation to have sex, she feels hot between her legs and knows that she has become wet. When he touches her there, he will discover this, and she doesn't know if this is good or bad, this is just how her body is reacting, and she doesn't intend telling him to go here or there, more slowly or more quickly. His hands are touching her armpits now, the hairs on her arms stand on end, and she feels like pushing his hands away, but it feels good, although perhaps it is pain she is feeling. She does the same to him and notices that the skin in his armpits has a different texture, perhaps because of the deodorant they both use, but what is she thinking of? She mustn't think. She must touch, that is all.

His fingers trace circles around her breast, like an animal watching. She wants them to move more quickly, to touch her nipples, because her thoughts are moving faster than his hands, but, perhaps knowing this, he provokes, lingers, takes an age to get there. Her nipples are hard now, he plays with them a little, and that causes more goose pimples, causes her to become hotter and wetter. Now he is moving across her belly, then down to her legs, her feet, he strokes his hands up and down her inner thigh, he feels the heat, but does not approach, his touch is soft, light, and the lighter it is the more intoxicating.

She does the same, her hands almost floating over his skin, touching only the hairs on his legs, and she too feels the heat when she approaches his genitals. Suddenly, it is as if she had mysteriously recovered her virginity, as if she were discovering a man's body for the first time. She touches his penis. It is not as hard as she imagined, and yet she is so wet, how unfair, but maybe a man needs more time, who knows.

And she begins to stroke it as only virgins know how, because prostitutes have long since forgotten. The man reacts, his penis begins to grow in her hands, and she slowly increases the pressure, knowing now where she should touch, more at the bottom than at the top, she must wrap her fingers around it, push the skin back, towards his body. Now he is excited, very excited, he touches the lips of her vagina, still very softly, and she feels like asking him to be more forceful, to put his fingers right inside. But he doesn't do that, he moistens the clitoris with a little of the liquid pouring from her womb, and again makes the same circular movements he made on her nipples. This man touches her exactly as she would touch herself.

One of his hands goes back to her breast; it feels so good, she wishes he would put his arms around her now. But, no, they are discovering the body, they have time, they need a lot of time. They could make love now; it would be the most natural thing in the world, and it might be good, but all this is so new, she needs to control herself, she does not want to spoil everything. She remembers the wine they drank on that first night, how they sipped it slowly, savouring each mouthful, how she felt it warming her and how it made her see the world differently and left her more at ease and more in touch with life.

She wants to drink that man too, and then she can forget forever the cheap wine that you gulp down and that makes you feel drunk, but always leaves you with a headache and an empty space in your soul.

She stops, slowly entwines her fingers with his, she hears a moan and would like to moan too, but she stops herself, she feels heat spreading throughout her body; the same thing must be happening to him. Without an orgasm, the energy disperses, travels to the brain, not letting her think of anything but going all the way, but this is what she wants, to stop, to stop halfway, to spread the pleasure through her whole body, to allow it to invade her mind, renewing her commitment and her desire, restoring her virginity.

She gently removes the blindfold from her own eyes and removes his too. She turns on the bedside lamp. Both are naked; they do not smile, they simply look at each other. I am love, I am music, she thinks. Let's dance.

But she doesn't say anything: they talk about something trivial, about when they will next meet, she suggests a date, perhaps in two days' time. He says he would like to invite her to an exhibition, but she hesitates. That would mean getting to know his world, his friends, and what would they say, what would they think.

She says no, but he realises that she really wants to say yes, and so he insists, using a few foolish arguments, but which are all part of the dance they are dancing now, and in the end she agrees, because that is what she would like. They arrange where to meet – in the same café where they met that first day? No, she says, Brazilians are very superstitious, and you must never meet in the same place where you first met, because that might close a cycle and bring everything to an end.

He says that he's glad she doesn't want to close that particular cycle. They decide to meet at a church from where you can see the whole city, and which is on the road to Santiago, part of the mysterious pilgrimage that the two of them have been on ever since they met.

From Maria's diary, on the eve of buying her ticket back to Brazil:

Once upon a time, there was a bird. He was adorned with two perfect wings and with glossy, colourful, marvellous feathers. In short, he was a creature made to fly about freely in the sky, bringing joy to everyone who saw him.

One day, a woman saw this bird and fell in love with him. She watched his flight, her mouth wide in amazement, her heart pounding, her eyes shining with excitement. She invited the bird to fly with her, and the two travelled across the sky in perfect harmony. She admired and venerated and celebrated that bird.

But then she thought: He might want to visit far-off mountains! And she was afraid, afraid that she would never feel the same way about any other bird. And she felt envy, envy for the bird's ability to fly.

And she felt alone.

And she thought: 'I'm going to set a trap. The next time the bird appears, he will never leave again.'

The bird, who was also in love, returned the following day, fell into the trap and was put in a cage.

She looked at the bird every day. There he was, the object of her passion, and she showed him to her friends, who said: 'Now you have everything you could possibly want.' However, a strange transformation began to take place: now that she had the bird and no longer needed to woo him, she began to lose interest. The bird, unable to fly and express the true meaning of his life, began to waste away and his feathers to lose their gloss; he grew ugly; and the woman no longer paid him any attention, except by feeding him and cleaning out his cage.

One day, the bird died. The woman felt terribly sad and spent all her time thinking about him. But she did not remember the cage, she thought only of the day when she had seen him for the first time, flying contentedly amongst the clouds.

If she had looked more deeply into herself, she would have realised that what had thrilled her about the bird was his freedom, the energy of his wings in motion, not his physical body.

Without the bird, her life too lost all meaning, and Death came knocking at her door. 'Why have you come?' she asked Death. 'So that you can fly once more with him across the sky,' Death replied. 'If you had allowed him to come and go, you would have loved and admired him even more; alas, you now need me in order to find him again.'

She started the day by doing something she had rehearsed over and over during all these past months: she went into a travel agent's and bought a ticket to Brazil for the date she had marked on her calendar, in two weeks' time.

From then on, Geneva would be the face of a man she loved and who had loved her. Rue de Berne would just be a name, a homage to Switzerland's capital city. She would remember her room, the lake, the French language, the crazy things a twenty-three-year-old woman (it had been her birthday the night before) is capable of – until she realises there is a limit.

She would not cage the bird, nor would she suggest he go with her to Brazil; he was the only truly pure thing that had happened to her. A bird like that must fly free and feed on nostalgia for the time when he flew alongside someone else. And she too was a bird; having Ralf Hart by her side would mean remembering forever her days at the Copacabana. And that was her past, not her future.

She decided to say 'goodbye' just once, when the moment came for her to leave, rather than have to suffer every time she thought: 'Soon I won't be here any more'. So she played a trick on her heart and, that morning, she walked around Geneva as if she had always known those streets, that hill, the road to Santiago, the Montblanc bridge, the bars she used to go to. She watched the seagulls flying over the river, the market traders taking down their stalls, people leaving their offices to go to lunch, noticed the colour and taste of the apple she was eating, the planes landing in the distance, the rainbow in the column of water rising up from the middle of the lake, the shy, concealed joy of passers-by, the looks she got, some full of desire, some expressionless. She had lived for nearly a year in a small town, like so many other small towns in the world, and if it hadn't been for the architecture peculiar to the place and the excessive number of banks, it could have been the interior of Brazil. There was a fair. There was a market. There were housewives haggling over prices. There were students who had skipped a class at school, on the excuse perhaps that their mother or their father was ill, and who were now strolling by the river, exchanging kisses. There were people who felt at home and people who felt foreign. There were tabloid newspapers full of scandals and respectable magazines for businessmen, who, however, were only ever to be seen reading the scandal sheets.

She went to the library to return the manual on farm management. She hadn't understood a word of it, but, at times when she felt she had lost control of herself and of her destiny, the book had served as a reminder of her objective in life. It had been a silent companion, with its plain yellow cover, its series of graphs, but, above all, it had been a lighthouse in the dark nights of recent weeks.

Always making plans for the future, and always being surprised by the present, she thought to herself. She felt she had discovered herself through independence, despair, love, pain, and back again to love – and she would like things to end there.

The oddest thing of all was that, while some of her work colleagues spoke of the wonder or the ecstasy of going to bed with certain men, she had never discovered anything either good or bad about herself through sex. She had not solved her problem, she could still not have an orgasm through penetration, and she had vulgarised the sexual act so much that she might never again find the 'embrace of recognition' – as Ralf Hart called it – or the fire and joy she sought.

Or perhaps (as she occasionally thought, and as mothers, fathers and romances all said) love was necessary if one was to experience pleasure in bed.

The normally serious librarian (and Maria's only friend, although she had never told her so) was in a good mood. She was having a bite to eat and invited her to share a sandwich. Maria thanked her and said that she had just eaten.

'You took a long time to read this.'

'I didn't understand a word.'

'Do you remember what you asked me once?'

No, she didn't, but when she saw the mischievous look on the other woman's face, she guessed. Sex.

'You know, after you came here in search of books on the subject, I decided to make a list of what we had. It wasn't much, and since we need to educate our young people in such matters, I ordered a few more books. At least, this way they won't need to learn about sex in that worst of all possible ways – by going with prostitutes.'

The librarian pointed to a pile of books in a corner, all discreetly covered in brown paper.

'I haven't had time to catalogue them yet, but I had a quick glance through and I was horrified by what I read.'

Maria could imagine what the woman was going to say: embarrassing positions, sadomasochism, things of that sort.

She had better tell her that she had to get back to work (she couldn't remember whether she had told her she worked in a bank or in a shop – lying made life so complicated, she was always forgetting what she had said).

She thanked her and was about to leave, when the other woman said:

'You'd be horrified too. Did you know, for example, that the clitoris is a recent invention?'

An invention? Recent? Just this week someone had touched hers, as if it had always been there and as if those hands knew the terrain they were exploring well, despite the total darkness.

'It was officially accepted in 1559, after a doctor, Realdo Columbo, published a book entitled *De re anatomica*. It was officially ignored for fifteen hundred years of the Christian era. Columbo describes it in his book as "a pretty and a useful thing". Can you believe it?'

They both laughed.

'Two years later, in 1561, another doctor, Gabriello Fallopio, said that he had "discovered" it. Imagine that! Two men – Italians, of course, who know about such things – arguing about who had officially added the clitoris to the history books!'

It was an interesting conversation, but Maria didn't want to think about these things, mainly because she could already feel the juices flowing and her vagina getting wet – just remembering his touch, the blindfolds, his hands moving over her body. No, she wasn't dead to sex; that man had managed to rescue her. It was good to be alive.

The librarian, however, was warming to her subject.

222

'Its "discovery" didn't mean it received any more respect, though.' The librarian seemed to have become an expert on clitorology, or whatever that science is called. 'The mutilations we read about now in certain African tribes, who still insist on removing the woman's right to sexual pleasure, are nothing new. In the nineteenth century, here in Europe, they were still performing operations to remove it, in the belief that in that small, insignificant part of the female anatomy lay the root of hysteria, epilepsy, adulterous tendencies and sterility.'

Maria held out her hand to say goodbye, but the librarian showed no signs of tiring.

'Worse still, dear Dr Freud, the founder of psychoanalysis, said that in a normal woman, the female orgasm should move from the clitoris to the vagina. His most faithful followers went further and said that if a woman's sexual pleasure remained concentrated in the clitoris, this was a sign of infantilism or, worse, bisexuality.

'And yet, as we all know, it is very difficult to have an orgasm just through penetration. It's good to have sex with a man, but pleasure lies in that little nub discovered by an Italian!'

Distracted, Maria realised that she had that problem diagnosed by Freud: she was still in the infantile stage, her orgasm had not moved to the vagina. Or was Freud wrong?

'And what do you think about the G-spot?'

'Do you know where it is?'

The other woman blushed and coughed, but managed to say:

'As you go in, on the first floor, the back window.'

Brilliant! She had described the vagina as if it were a building! Perhaps she had read that explanation in a book for young girls, to say that if someone knocks on the door and comes in, you'll discover a whole universe inside your own body. Whenever she masturbated, she preferred to concentrate on her G-spot rather than on the clitoris, since the latter made her feel rather uncomfortable, a pleasure mingled with real pain, rather troubling.

She always went straight to the first floor, to the back window!

Seeing that the librarian was clearly never going to stop talking, perhaps because she had discovered in Maria an accomplice to her own lost sexuality, she gave a wave of her hand and left, trying to concentrate on whatever nonsense came into her head, because this was not a day to think about farewells, clitorises, restored virginities or G-spots. She focused on what was going on around her – bells ringing, dogs barking, a tram rattling over the tracks, footsteps, her own breathing, the signs offering everything under the sun.

She did not feel like going back to the Copacabana, and yet she felt an obligation to work until the end, although she had no real idea why – after all, she had saved enough money. She could spend the afternoon doing some shopping, talking to the bank manager, who was a client of hers, but who had promised to help her manage her savings, having a cup of coffee somewhere, sending off the clothes that wouldn't fit into her suitcases. It was strange, for some reason, she was feeling rather sad; perhaps because it was still another two weeks before she would leave, and she needed to get through that time, to look at the city with different eyes and feel glad for what she had experienced there.

She came to a crossroads where she had been hundreds of time before; you could see the lake from there and the water spout, and, on the far pavement, in the middle of the public gardens, the lovely floral clock, one of the city's symbols ... and that clock would not allow her to lie, because ...

Suddenly, time and the world stood still.

What was this story she had been telling herself since the morning, something about her recently restored virginity?

The world seemed frozen, that second would never end, she was face to face with something very serious and very important in her life, she could not just forget about it, she could not do as she did with her night-time dreams, which she always promised herself she would write down and which she never did ...

'Don't think about anything! The world has stopped. What's going on?'

ENOUGH!

The bird, the lovely story about the bird she had just written – was it about Ralf Hart?

No, it was about her!

FULL STOP!

It was 11:11 in the morning, and she was frozen in that moment. She was a foreigner inside her own body, she was rediscovering her recently restored virginity, but its rebirth was so fragile that if she stayed there, it would be lost forever. She had experienced Heaven perhaps, certainly Hell, but the Adventure was coming to an end. She couldn't wait two weeks, ten days, one week – she needed to leave now, because, as she stood looking at the floral clock, with tourists taking pictures of it and children playing all around, she had just found out why she was sad.

And the reason was this: she didn't want to go back.

And the reason she didn't want to go back wasn't Ralf Hart, Switzerland or Adventure. The real reason couldn't have been simpler: money.

Money! A special piece of paper, decorated in sombre colours, which everyone agreed was worth something – and she believed it, everyone believed it – until you took a pile of that paper to a bank, a respectable, traditional, highly confidential Swiss bank and asked: 'Could I buy back a few hours of my life?' 'No, madam, we don't sell, we only buy.'

Maria was woken from her delirium by the sound of screeching brakes, a motorist shouting, and a smiling old gentleman, speaking English, telling her to step back onto the pavement – the pedestrian light was red.

'But this can't be exactly an earth-shattering discovery. Everyone must feel what I feel. They must know.'

But they didn't. She looked around her. People were walking along, heads down, hurrying off to work, to school, to the employment agency, to Rue de Berne, telling themselves: 'I can wait a little longer. I have a dream, but there's no need to realise it today, besides, I need to earn some money.' Of course, everyone spoke ill of her profession, but, basically, it was all a question of selling her time, like everyone else. Doing things she didn't want to do, like everyone else. Putting up with horrible people, like everyone else. Handing over her precious body and her precious soul in the name of a future that never arrived, like everyone else. Saying that she still didn't have enough, like everyone else. Waiting just a little bit longer, like everyone else. Waiting so that she could earn just a little bit more, postponing the realisation of her dreams; she was too busy right now, she had a great opportunity ahead of her, loyal clients who were waiting for her, who could pay between three hundred and fifty and one thousand francs a session.

And for the first time in her life, despite all the good things she could buy with the money she might earn – who knows, she might only have to work another year – she decided consciously, lucidly and deliberately to let an opportunity pass her by.

Maria waited for the light to change, she crossed the road and paused in front of the floral clock; she thought of Ralf, saw again the look of desire in his eyes on the night when she had slipped off the top half of her dress, felt his hands touching her breasts, her sex, her face, and she became wet; and as she looked at the vast column of water in the distance, without even having to touch any part of her own body, she had an orgasm right there, in front of everyone.

Not that anyone noticed; they were all far too busy.

227

Nyah, the only one of her work colleagues with whom she had a relationship that could be described as friendship, called her over as soon as she came in. She was sitting with an oriental gentleman, and they were both laughing.

'Look at this,' she said to Maria. 'Look what he wants me to do with him!'

The oriental gentleman gave a knowing look and, still smiling, opened the lid of what looked like a cigar box. Milan was watching from a distance in case it contained syringes or drugs. It did not, it was something that even he didn't know quite what to do with, but it wasn't anything very special.

'It looks like something from the last century!' said Maria.

'It is,' said the oriental gentleman indignantly. 'It's over a hundred years old and it cost a fortune.'

What Maria saw was a series of valves, a handle, electric circuits, small metal contacts and batteries. It looked like the inside of an ancient radio, with two wires sticking out, at the ends of which were small glass rods, about the thickness of a finger. It certainly didn't look like something that had cost a fortune.

'How does it work?'

Nyah didn't like Maria's question. Although she trusted Maria, people could change from one moment to the next, and she might have her eye on her client.

'He's already explained. It's the Violet Rod.'

And turning to the oriental man, she suggested that they leave, because she had decided to accept his invitation. However, the man seemed pleased that his toy should have aroused such interest.

'Around 1900, when the first batteries came onto the market, traditional medicine started experimenting with electricity to see if it could cure mental illness or hysteria. It was also used to get rid of spots and to stimulate the skin. You see these two ends? Well, they were placed here,' he indicated his temples, 'and the battery created the same sort of static electricity that you get in Switzerland when the air's very dry.'

Static electricity was something that never happened in Brazil, but was very common in Switzerland. Maria had discovered it one day when she opened the door of a taxi; she had heard a crack and received a shock. She thought there must be something wrong with the car and had complained, saying that she wasn't going to pay the fare, and the driver had insulted her and told her she was stupid. He was right; it wasn't the car, it was the dry air. After receiving several more shocks, she began to be afraid of touching anything made of metal, until she discovered in a supermarket a bracelet she could wear that discharged the electricity accumulated in the body.

She turned to the man:

'But that's really nasty.'

Nyah was getting more and more irritated by Maria's remarks. In order to avoid future conflicts with her only possible friend, she kept her arm around the man's shoulder, thus leaving no room for doubt as to who he belonged to.

230

'It depends where you put it,' said the man, laughing loudly.

He turned the little handle and the two rods seemed to turn violet. He quickly placed them on the two women; there was a crack, but the shock was more ticklish than painful.

Milan came over.

'Would you mind not using that in here, please.'

The man put the rods back inside the box. Nyah seized the moment and suggested that they go straight to the hotel. The man seemed rather disappointed, since the new arrival seemed far more interested in his machine than the woman who was now suggesting they go back to his hotel. He put on his jacket and stowed the box away inside a leather briefcase, saying:

'They've started making them again now; they've become quite fashionable amongst people in search of special pleasures. But you'd only find ones like this in rare medical collections, museums and antique shops.'

Milan and Maria just stood there, not knowing what to say.

'Have you ever seen one before?'

'Not like that, no. It probably did cost a fortune, but then he's a top executive with an oil company ... I've seen modern ones, though.'

'What do they do with them?'

'The man puts them inside his body ... and then asks the woman to turn the handle. He gets an electric shock inside.'

'Couldn't he do that on his own?'

'You can do most kinds of sexual activity on your own, but if they stopped believing that it was more fun with another person, my bar would go bankrupt and you would have to find work in a greengrocer's shop. By the way, your special client said that he would be here tonight, so make sure you turn down any other offers.'

'Oh, I will, including his. I came to say goodbye. I'm leaving.'

Milan appeared not to react.

'Is it the painter?'

'No, it's the Copacabana. There's a limit to everything, and I reached mine this morning when I was looking at that floral clock near the lake.'

'And what is the limit?'

'The price of a farm in the interior of Brazil. I know I could earn more money, that I could work for another year – after all, what difference would it make?

'Well, I know what difference it would make; I would be caught in this trap forever, just as you are and the clients are, the businessmen, the air stewards, the talent scouts, the record company executives, the many men I have known, to whom I have sold my time and which they can't sell back to me. If I stay another day, I'll be here for another year, and if I stay another year, I'll never leave.'

Milan nodded discreetly, as if he understood and agreed with everything she had said, although he couldn't actually say anything, for fear of infecting all the other girls who worked for him. He was a good man, and although he didn't give her his blessing, neither did he try to convince Maria that she was wrong.

She thanked him and asked for a drink – a glass of champagne, she couldn't stand another fruit juice cocktail.

She could drink now that she wasn't working. Milan told her to phone him if ever she needed anything; she would always be welcome.

She made to pay for the drink, and he said it was on the house. She accepted: she had, after all, given that house a great deal more than one drink.

From Maria's diary, when she got home:

I don't remember exactly when, but one Sunday recently, I decided to go to church to attend mass. After some time, I realised that I was in the wrong church – it was a Protestant church.

I was about to leave, but the vicar was just beginning his sermon, and I thought it would be rude to get up at that point, and it was a real blessing, because that day I heard things I very much needed to hear.

He said something like:

'In all the languages in the world, there is the same proverb: "What the eyes don't see, the heart doesn't grieve over." Well, I say that there isn't an ounce of truth in it. The further off they are, the closer to the heart are all those feelings that we try to repress and forget. If we're in exile, we want to store away every tiny memory of our roots. If we're far from the person we love, everyone we pass in the street reminds us of them.

'The gospels and all the sacred texts of all religions were written in exile, in search of God's understanding, of the faith that moves whole peoples, of the

pilgrimage of souls wandering the face of the Earth. Our ancestors did not know, as we do not know, what the Divinity expects from our lives – and it is out of that doubt that books are written, pictures painted, because we don't want to forget who we are – nor can we.'

At the end of the service, I went up to him and thanked him: I said that I was a stranger in a strange land, and I thanked him for reminding me that what the eyes don't see, the heart does grieve over. And my heart has grieved so much, that today I'm leaving.

She picked up her two suitcases and put them on the bed; they had always been there, waiting for the day when everything would come to an end. She had imagined that she would fill them with presents, new clothes, photographs of snow and of the great European capitals, souvenirs of a happy time when she had lived in the safest and most generous country in the world. She had a few new clothes, it was true, and a few photos taken in the snow that fell one day in Geneva, but apart from that, nothing was as she had imagined it would be.

She had arrived with the dream of earning lots of money, learning about life and who she was, buying a farm for her parents, finding a husband, and bringing her family over to see where she lived. She was returning with just enough money to realise one of those dreams, without ever having visited the mountains and, worse still, a stranger to herself. But she was happy; she knew the time had come to stop.

Not many people do.

She had had only four adventures – being a dancer in a cabaret, learning French, working as a prostitute and falling hopelessly in love. How many people can boast of experiencing so much excitement in one year? She was happy, despite the sadness, and that sadness had a name: it wasn't prostitution, or Switzerland or money – it was Ralf Hart. Although she had never acknowledged it to herself, deep down, she would like to have married him, that man who was now waiting for her in a church, ready to take her off to see his friends, his paintings, his world.

She considered standing him up and getting a room in a hotel near the airport, since the flight left early the next morning; from now on, every minute spent by his side would be a year of suffering in the future, for everything she could have said to him and didn't, for her memories of his hands, his voice, his loving support, and his stories.

She opened one suitcase and took out the little carriage from the electric train set that he had given her on that first night in his house. She looked at it for a few minutes, then threw it in the bin; it didn't deserve to go to Brazil, and it had proved useless and unfair to the child who had always wanted it.

No, she wouldn't go to the church; he might ask her something about tomorrow, and if she was honest and told him that she was leaving, he would beg her to stay and promise her everything in order not to lose her at that moment, he would openly declare all the love he had already shown to her during the time they had spent together. But their relationship was based on freedom, and no other sort of relationship would work – perhaps that was the only reason they loved each other, because they knew they did not need each other. Men always take fright when a woman says: 'I need you', and Maria wanted to take away with her the image of a Ralf Hart who was utterly in love and utterly hers, and ready to do anything for her.

She still had time to decide whether or not to go and meet him; at the moment, she needed to concentrate on more practical matters. She looked at all the things she couldn't pack and which she had no idea what to do with. She decided that the owner could decide on their fate when he came to check the apartment and found all the household appliances in the kitchen, the pictures bought in a second-hand market, the towels and the bedclothes. She couldn't take any of that with her to Brazil, even though her parents had more need of them than any Swiss beggar; they would always remind her of everything she had risked.

She left the apartment and went to the bank and asked to withdraw all her money. The manager – who had been to bed with her in the past – said that this really wasn't a good idea, since her francs would continue earning money and she could receive the interest in Brazil. Besides, what if she were mugged, that would mean months of work wasted. Maria hesitated for a moment, thinking – as she always did – that he really was trying to help. However, after reflecting for a moment, she concluded that the point of the money was not that it should be transformed into more paper, but into a farm, a home for her parents, a few cattle and a lot more work.

She withdrew every last centime, put it in a small bag she had bought specially for the occasion and attached it to a belt beneath her clothes.

She went to the travel agency, praying that she would have the courage to go through with her decision. When she said she wanted to get a different flight, she was told that if she went on tomorrow's flight, she would have to change planes in Paris. That didn't matter – all she needed was to get far enough away from there before she had second thoughts.

She walked to one of the bridges and bought an ice cream, even though the weather had started to get cold again, and she took one last look at Geneva. Everything seemed different to her, as if she had just arrived and needed to visit the museums, the historical monuments, the fashionable bars and restaurants. It's odd how, when you live in a city, you always postpone getting to know it and usually end up never knowing it at all.

She thought she would feel happy because she was going home, but she wasn't. She thought she would feel sad because she was leaving a city that had treated her so well, but she didn't. The only thing she could do now was to shed a few tears, feeling rather afraid of herself, an intelligent young woman, who had everything going for her, but who tended to make the wrong decisions.

She just hoped that this time she was right.

The church was completely empty when she went in, and she was able to examine in silence the splendid stained-glass windows, lit from outside by the light of a day washed clean by last night's storm. Before her stood an empty cross; she was confronted not by an instrument of torture, by the bloodied body of a dying man, but by a symbol of resurrection, in which the instrument of torture had lost all its meaning, its terror, its importance. She remembered the whip on that night of thunder and lightning; it was the same thing. 'Dear God, what am I saying?'

She was pleased too not to see any images of suffering saints, covered in bloodstains and open wounds – this was simply a place where people gathered to worship something they could not understand.

She stood in front of the monstrance, in which was kept the body of a Jesus in whom she still believed, although she had not thought about him for a long time. She knelt down and promised God, the Virgin, Jesus and all the saints that whatever happened that day, she would not change her mind and would leave anyway. She made this promise because she knew love's traps all too well, and knew how easily they can change a woman's mind.

Shortly afterwards, she felt a hand touch her shoulder and she inclined her head so that her face rested on the hand.

'How are you?'

'I'm fine,' she said in a voice without a trace of anxiety in it. 'I'm fine. Let's go and have a coffee.'

They left the church hand-in-hand, as if they were two lovers meeting again after a long time. They kissed in public, and a few people shot them scandalised looks; but they both smiled at the unease they were causing and at the desires they were provoking by their scandalous behaviour, because they knew that, in fact, those people wished they could be doing the same thing. That was the real scandal.

They went into a café which was the same as all the others, but that afternoon, it was different, because they were there together and because they loved each other. They talked about Geneva, the difficulties of the French language, the stained-glass windows in the church, the evils of smoking – both of them smoked and hadn't the slightest intention of giving up.

She insisted on paying for the coffee and he accepted. They went to the exhibition and she got to know his world: the artists, the rich who looked richer than they actually were, the millionaires who looked poor, the people discussing things she had never even heard about. They all liked her and praised her French; they asked about Carnival, football, Brazilian music. They were nice, polite, kind, charming.

When they left, he said that he would come to the club that night to see her. She asked him not to, she had the night off and would like to invite him out to supper.

He accepted and they said goodbye, arranging to meet at his house before going to have supper at a delightful restaurant in the little square in Cologny, which they had often driven past in the taxi, and where she had always wanted to stop, but had never asked to.

Then Maria remembered her one friend and decided to go to the library to tell her that she would not be coming back.

She got caught up in the traffic for what seemed like an eternity, until the Kurds had (once more!) finished their demonstration and the cars could move freely again. Now, however, she was the mistress of her own time, and it didn't matter.

By the time she reached the library, it was just about to close.

'Forgive me if I'm being too personal, but I haven't anyone else, any woman friend, I can talk to about certain things,' said the librarian as soon as Maria came in.

She didn't have any women friends? After spending her whole life in the same place and meeting all kinds of people at work, did she really have no one she could talk to? Maria had found someone like herself, or, rather, like everyone else.

'I was thinking about what I read about the clitoris ...'

Didn't she ever think about anything else!

'It's just that, although I used to enjoy sex with my husband, I always found it very difficult to reach orgasm during intercourse. Do you think that's normal?'

'Do you find it normal that there are daily demonstrations by Kurds? That women in love run away from their Prince Charming? That people dream about farms rather than love? That men and women sell their time, but can never buy it back again? And yet, all these things happen, so it really doesn't matter what I believe or don't believe; all these things are normal. Everything that goes against Nature, against our most intimate desires, is normal in our eyes, even though it's an aberration in God's eyes. We seek out our own inferno, we spend millennia building it, and after all that effort, we are now able to live in the worst possible way.'

She looked at the woman standing in front of her and, for the first time, she asked what her name was (she only knew her surname). Her name was Heidi, she was married for thirty years and never – never! – during that time had she asked herself if it was normal not to have an orgasm during intercourse with her husband.

'I don't know if I should have read all those things! Perhaps it would have been better to live in ignorance, believing that a faithful husband, an apartment with a view of the lake, three children and a job in the public sector were all that a woman could hope for. Now, ever since you arrived, and since I read the first book, I'm obsessed with what my life has become. Is everyone the same?'

'I can guarantee you that they are.' And standing before that woman who was asking her advice, Maria felt herself to be very wise.

'Would you like me to give you details?'

Maria nodded.

'You're obviously too young to understand these things, but that's precisely why I would like to share a little of my life with you, so that you don't make the same mistakes I did.

'But why is it that my husband never noticed my clitoris? He assumed that the orgasm happened in the vagina, and I found it really, really difficult to pretend something that he imagined I must be feeling. Of course, I did experience pleasure, but a different kind of pleasure. It was only when the friction was on the upper part ... do you know what I mean?'

'I know.'

'And now I know why. It's in there,' she pointed to a book on her desk, whose title Maria couldn't see. 'There are lots of nerve endings that connect the clitoris and the G-spot and which are crucial to orgasm. But men think that penetration is all. Do you know what the G-spot is?'

'Yes, we talked about it the other day,' said Maria, slipping into the role of Innocent Girl. 'As you go in, on the first floor, the back window.'

'That's right!' And the librarian's eyes lit up. 'Just you ask how many of your male friends have heard of it. None of them! It's absurd. But just as an Italian discovered the clitoris, the G-spot is a twentieth-century discovery! Soon it will be in all the headlines, and then no one will be able to ignore it any longer! Have you any idea what revolutionary times we're living in?'

Maria glanced at her watch, and Heidi realised that she would have to talk fast, in order to teach this pretty young woman that all women have the right to be happy and fulfilled, in order that the next generation should benefit from all these extraordinary scientific discoveries.

'Dr Freud didn't agree because he wasn't a woman and, since he experienced his orgasm through his penis, he felt that women must, therefore, experience pleasure in their vagina. We've got to go back to basics, to what has always given us pleasure: the clitoris and the G-spot! Very few women enjoy a satisfactory sexual relationship, so if you have difficulty in getting the pleasure you deserve, let me suggest something: change position. Make your lover lie down and you stay on top; your clitoris will strike his body harder and you – not he – will be getting the stimulus you need. Or, rather, the stimulus you deserve!'

Maria, meanwhile, was only pretending that she wasn't listening to the conversation. So she wasn't the only one! She didn't have a sexual problem, it was all just a question of anatomy! She felt like kissing the librarian, as if a gigantic weight had been lifted off her heart. How good to have discovered this while she was still young! What a marvellous day she was having! Heidi gave a conspiratorial smile.

'They may not know it, but we have an erection too. The clitoris becomes erect!'

'They' presumably meant men. Since this was such an intimate conversation, Maria decided to risk a question:

'Have you ever had an affair?'

The librarian looked shocked. Her eyes gave off a kind of sacred fire, she blushed scarlet, though whether out of rage or shame it was impossible to tell. After a while, though, the battle between telling the truth or pretending ended. She simply changed the subject.

'Getting back to our erection, to our clitoris, did you know that it became rigid?'

'Yes, I've known that ever since I was a child.'

Heidi seemed disappointed. Perhaps she had just never noticed. Nevertheless, she resolved to go on:

'Anyway, apparently, if you rub your finger round it, without touching the actual tip, you can experience even more intense pleasure. So take note! Men who do respect a woman's body immediately touch the tip, not knowing that this can sometimes be quite painful, don't you agree? So, after your first or second encounter, take control of the situation: get on top, decide how and when pressure should be applied, and increase and decrease the rhythm as you see fit. According to the book I'm reading, a frank conversation about it might also be a good idea.'

'Did you ever have a frank conversation with your husband?'

Again, Heidi avoided this direct question, saying that things were different then. Now she was more interested in sharing her intellectual experiences.

'Try to think of your clitoris as the hands of a clock and ask your partner to move it back and forth between eleven and one, do you understand?'

Yes, she knew what the woman was talking about and didn't entirely agree, although the book wasn't far from the truth. As soon as she mentioned the word 'clock', though, Maria glanced at her watch, and explained that she had really come to say goodbye, her job placement had come to an end. The woman seemed not to hear her.

'Would you like to borrow this book about the clitoris?'

'No, thanks. I've got other things to think about at the moment.'

'And you don't want to borrow anything else?'

'No. I'm going back to my own country, but I just wanted to thank you for always having treated me with such respect and understanding. Perhaps we'll meet again some time.'

They shook hands and wished each other much happiness.

Heidi waited until the girl had left, then thumped the desk. Why hadn't she seized the opportunity to share something which, the way things were going, would probably go to the grave with her? Since the girl had had the courage to ask if she had ever betrayed her husband, why had she not answered, now that she was discovering a new world in which women were finally acknowledging how difficult it was to achieve a vaginal orgasm?

'Oh well, it doesn't matter. The world isn't just about sex.'

No, it wasn't the most important thing in the world, but it was still important. She looked around her; most of the thousands of books surrounding her were love stories. It was always the same: someone meets someone, falls in love, loses them and finds them again. There are souls speaking unto souls, there are distant places, adventures, sufferings, anxieties, but very rarely anyone saying: 'Excuse me, sir, but why don't you try acquiring a better understanding of the female body?' Why didn't books talk openly about that?

Perhaps people weren't really interested. Men would always go looking for novelty; they were still the troglodyte hunter, obeying the reproductive instinct of the human race. And what about women? In her personal experience, the desire to have a good orgasm with one's partner lasted only for the first few years; then the frequency of orgasms diminished, but no one talked about it, because every woman thought it was her problem alone. And so they lied,

247

pretending that they found their husband's desire to make love every night oppressive. And by lying, they left other women feeling worried.

They turned their thoughts to other things: children, cooking, timetables, housework, bills to pay, their husband's affairs – which they tolerated – holidays abroad during which they were more concerned with their children than with themselves, their complicity, or even love, but no sex.

She should have been more open with that young Brazilian woman, who seemed to her an innocent creature, old enough to be her daughter, and still incapable of understanding what the world was like. An immigrant, far from home, working hard at a boring job, waiting for a man she could marry, and with whom she could fake a few orgasms, find security, reproduce this mysterious human race, and then forget all about such things as orgasms, the clitoris or the G-spot (which was only discovered in the twentieth century!!). Being a good wife, a good mother, making sure there was nothing lacking in the home, masturbating occasionally in secret, thinking about some man who had passed her in the street and looked at her longingly. Keeping up appearances – why was the world so concerned with appearances?

That is why she had not replied to the question: 'Have you ever had an affair?'

These things go with you to the grave, she thought. Her husband had been the only man in her life, although sex was now a thing of the remote past. He had been an excellent companion, honest, generous and good-humoured, and had struggled to bring up the family and to keep all those who worked with him happy. He was the ideal man that all women dream of, and that is precisely why she felt so bad when she thought of how she had one day desired and been with another man.

She remembered how they had met. She was coming back from the small mountain town of Davos, when all the train services were interrupted for some hours by an avalanche. She phoned home so that no one would be worried, bought a few magazines and prepared for a long wait at the station.

That was when she noticed the man sitting next to her, along with his rucksack and sleeping bag. He had greying hair and sunburned skin, and was the only person in the station who didn't seem concerned about the absence of any trains; on the contrary, he was smiling and looking around him for someone to talk to. Heidi opened one of the magazines, but – ah, sweet mystery of life! – her eyes happened to catch his and she didn't manage to look away quickly enough to avoid him coming over to her.

Before she could – politely – say that she really needed to finish reading an important article, he began to talk. He told her that he was a writer and was returning from a meeting in Davos and that the delay would mean him missing his flight home. When they got to Geneva, would she mind helping him find a hotel?

Heidi was watching him: how could anyone be so cheerful about missing a plane and having to wait in an uncomfortable train station until things were sorted out?

The man began talking to her as if they were old friends. He told her about his travels, about the mystique of literary creation and, to her horror, about all the women he had known and loved in his lifetime. Heidi merely nodded and let him talk. Occasionally he would apologise for talking so much and ask her to tell him something about herself, but all she could say was: 'Oh, I'm just an ordinary person, nothing very special.'

Suddenly, she found herself hoping that the train would never arrive; the conversation was so enthralling; she was discovering things that she had only encountered before in fiction. And since she would never see him again, she got up her nerve and (quite why she could never say) began asking him about subjects of particular interest to her. Her marriage was going through a rough patch, her husband was very demanding of her time, and Heidi wanted to know what she could do to make him happy. The man offered her some interesting explanations, told her a story, but didn't seem very comfortable talking about her husband.

'You're a very interesting woman,' he said, something that no one had said to her for years.

Heidi didn't know how to react; he saw her embarrassment and immediately started talking about deserts, mountains, lost cities, women with veiled faces or bare midriffs, about warriors, pirates and wise men.

The train arrived. They sat down next to each other, and she was no longer a married woman who lived in a chalet looking out over the lake and had three children to bring up, she was an adventurer arriving in Geneva for the first time. She looked at the mountains and the river and felt glad to be sitting beside a man who wanted to go to bed with her (because that's all men think about) and who was doing his best to impress her. She wondered how many other men had felt the same, but to whom she had never given the slightest encouragement; that morning, however, the world had changed, and she was suddenly a thirty-eight-year-old adolescent, dazzled by this man's attempts to seduce her; it was the best feeling in the world.

In the premature autumn of her life, when she thought she had everything she could possibly want, this man appeared at the train station and walked straight into her life without first asking permission. They got off at Geneva and she showed him a hotel (a cheap one, he said, because he should have left that morning and didn't have much money on him for another night in exorbitantly expensive Switzerland); he asked her to go up to the room with him, to see if everything was in order. Heidi knew what to expect, and nevertheless, she accepted his proposal. They shut the door, they kissed each other with wild abandon, he tore off her clothes and – dear God! – he knew all about the female body, because he had known the sufferings and frustrations of so many women.

They made love all afternoon and only when evening fell did the charm dissipate, and she said the words she would have preferred not to have said:

'I must go home, my husband's expecting me.'

He lit a cigarette and they lay in silence for a few moments, and neither of them said 'goodbye'. Heidi got up and left without looking back, knowing that, whatever either of them might say, no word or phrase would make any sense.

She would never see him again, but, for a few hours, in the autumn of her despair, she had ceased to be a faithful wife, housewife, loving mother, exemplary public servant and constant friend, and reverted to being simply a woman.

For a few days, her husband kept saying that she seemed different, either happier or sadder, he couldn't quite put his finger on it. A week later, everything was back to normal.

'What a shame I didn't tell that young woman,' she thought. 'Not that she would have understood, she still lives in a world in which people are faithful and vows of love are forever.'

From Maria's diary:

I don't know what he must have thought when he opened the door that night and saw me standing there, carrying two suitcases.

'Don't worry,' I said. 'I'm not moving in. Shall we go to supper?'

He didn't say anything, just helped me in with my luggage. Then, without saying 'what's going on?' or 'how lovely to see you', he simply put his arms around me and started kissing me and touching my body, my breasts, my crotch, as if he had been waiting for this a long time and was now afraid that the moment would never come.

He pulled off my jacket and my dress, leaving me naked, and there in the hall, without any ritual or preparation, without even time to say what would be good and what bad, with the cold wind blowing in under the front door, we made love for the first time. I thought perhaps I should tell him to stop, so that we could find somewhere more comfortable, so that we could have time to explore the immense world of our sensuality, but, at the same time, I wanted him inside me, because he was the man I had never possessed and would never possess again. That is why I could love him with all my energy, and have, at least for one night, what I'd never had before and what I would possibly never have again.

He lay me down on the floor and entered me before I was aroused and ready, but the pain didn't bother me; on the contrary, I liked it like that, because he obviously understood that I was his and that he didn't need to ask permission. I wasn't there in order to teach him anything or to prove that I was more sensitive or more passionate than other women, I was there to say yes, you're welcome, that I too had been waiting for this, that I was pleased about his total disregard for the rules we had created between us and that he was now demanding that we should be guided solely by our instincts, male and female.

We were in the most conventional of positions – me underneath him, with my legs spread, and him on top of me, moving in and out, while I looked at him, with no desire to pretend or to moan or to do anything, just wanting to keep my eyes open so that I could remember every second, watch his face changing, his hands grabbing my hair, his mouth biting me, kissing me. No preliminaries, no caresses, no preparations, no sophistication, just him inside me and me inside his soul.

He came and went, quickening and slowing the rhythm, stopping sometimes to look at me too, but he didn't ask if I was enjoying it, because he knew that this was the only way our souls could communicate at that moment. The rhythm increased, and I knew that the eleven minutes were coming to an end, and I wanted them to last forever, because it was so good – ah, dear God, it was good – to be possessed and not to possess! And we had our eyes wide open all the time, until I noticed that at one point we were no longer seeing clearly any more and we seemed to move into a dimension in which I was the great mother, the universe, the beloved, the sacred prostitute of the ancient rituals that he had told me about over wine and beside an open fire. I saw that he was about to come, and his arms gripped mine, his movements increased in intensity, and it was then that he shouted – he didn't moan, he didn't grind his teeth, he shouted. He yelled. He roared like an animal! A thought flashed through my mind that the neighbours might call the police, but it didn't matter, and I felt immense pleasure, because this was how it had been since the beginning of time, when the first man met the first woman and they made love for the first time: they shouted.

Then his body collapsed onto mine, and I don't know how long we stayed there, our arms around each other; I stroked his hair as I had done only once before, on the night when we locked ourselves up in the darkness of the hotel room; I felt his racing heart gradually slow to its normal rate; his hands began delicately to move up and down my arms, making all the hairs on my body prickle.

He must have had a practical thought – the weight of his body on mine – because he rolled over, took my hand, and we lay there staring up at the ceiling and the chandelier with its three light bulbs lit.

'Good evening,' I said.

He drew me over so that my head was resting on his chest. For a long time, he just stroked me, and then he said 'Good evening' too.

'The neighbours must have heard everything,' I said, not knowing quite what to say next, because saying 'I love you' at that juncture didn't make much sense: he knew that already, and so did I.

'There's a terrific draught from under the door,' he said, when he could have said: 'Good!'

'Let's go into the kitchen.'

We got up and I saw that he hadn't even taken off his trousers, he was dressed just as I had found him, only with his penis exposed. I put my jacket over my bare shoulders. We went into the kitchen; he made some coffee; he smoked two cigarettes and I smoked one. Sitting at the table, he said 'thank you' with his eyes, and I replied 'thank you too', but our mouths remained shut.

He eventually got up the courage to ask about the suitcases.

'I'm flying back to Brazil tomorrow at midday.'

A woman knows when a man is important to her. Are men capable of that kind of realisation? Or would I have to say: 'I love you', 'I'd like to stay here with you', 'ask me to stay'.

'Don't go.' Yes, he had understood that he could say that to me.

'I have to. I made a promise.'

Because, if I hadn't, he might think that this was all going to last forever. And it wasn't; it was part of the dream of a young woman from the interior of a far-off country, who goes to the big city (well, not that big really), encounters all kinds of difficulties, but finds the man who loves her. So this was the happy ending to all the difficult times I had been through, and whenever I remembered my life in Europe, I would end with the story of a man passionately in love with me, and who would always be mine, because I had visited his soul.

Ah, Ralf, you have no idea how much I love you. I think that perhaps we always fall in love the very first instant we see the man of our dreams, even though, at the time, reason may be telling us otherwise, and we may fight against that instinct, hoping against hope that we won't win, until there comes a point when we allow ourselves to be vanquished by our feelings. That happened on the night when I walked barefoot in the park, cold and in pain, but knowing how much you loved me.

Yes, I love you very much, as I have never loved another man, and that is precisely why I am leaving, because, if I stayed, the dream would become reality, the desire to possess, to want your life to be mine ... in short, all the things that transform love into slavery. It's best left like this – a dream. We have to be careful what we take from a country, or from life.

'You didn't have an orgasm,' he said, trying to change the subject, to be careful and not to force the situation. He was afraid of losing me, and was thinking that he still had all night to make me change my mind.

'No, I didn't, but I had an enormous amount of pleasure.'

'But it would have been better if you'd had an orgasm too.'

'I could have pretended, just to please you, but you don't deserve that. Ralf Hart, you are a man in the most beautiful, intense sense of the word. You've supported me and helped me, you've let me support and help you, without there being any humiliation on either side. Yes, it would have been good to have an orgasm, but I didn't. But I loved the cold floor, your warm body, the force with which you entered me.

'I went to take back my library books today, and the librarian asked if I talked to my partner about sex. I felt like saying: Which partner? What sort of sex do you mean? But she didn't deserve that; she's always been so sweet to me.

'I've really only had two partners since I came to Geneva: one who awoke the worst in me, because I let him and even begged him to. The other one, you, who made me feel part of the world again. I would like to be able to teach you where to touch my body, how much pressure to apply, for how long, and I know you would take this not as a criticism, but as another way

257

to improve communication between our souls. *The art of love is like your painting, it requires technique, patience, and, above all, practice by the couple. It requires boldness, the courage to go beyond what people conventionally call "making love".*'

The teacher in me was back, and I didn't want that, but Ralf knew how to take control of the situation. Instead of agreeing with me, he lit his third cigarette in less than half an hour and said:

'Firstly, you're staying here tonight.'

It wasn't a request, it was an order.

'Secondly, we're going to make love again, but with less anxiety this time and more desire. And finally, I'd like you to understand men better too.

Understand men better? I spent every night with them, whites, blacks, Asians, Jews, Muslims, Catholics, Buddhists. Didn't Ralf know that?

I felt lighter; I was so pleased that the conversation had shifted into being a discussion. At one point, I even considered asking God's forgiveness and breaking my promise. But reality returned, telling me to remember to preserve my dream intact and not to fall into destiny's traps.

'Yes, to understand men better,' said Ralf again, seeing the doubtful look on my face. 'You talk about your female sexuality, about helping me to find my way around your body, to be patient, to take time. I agree, but has it occurred to you that we're different, at least in matters of time? You should complain to God about that.

'When we met, I asked you to teach me about sex, because I had lost all my sexual desire. Do you know why? Because after a certain age, every sexual relationship I had ended in tedium and frustration, because I realised how difficult it was to give the women I loved the same amount of pleasure they gave me.'

I didn't like the sound of 'the women I loved', but I feigned indifference and lit a cigarette.

'I didn't have the courage to ask: show me your body. But when I met you, I saw your light, and I loved you at once, and I thought that, at this stage in my life, I had nothing to lose by being honest with myself and with the woman I wanted to have by my side.'

My cigarette tasted delicious, and I would have liked him to offer me some wine, but I didn't want to break the thread of the conversation.

'Why is it that men only think about sex, instead of doing as you did with me and finding out how I feel?'

'Who said we only think about sex? On the contrary, we spend years of our life trying to convince ourselves that sex is actually important to us. We learn about love from prostitutes or virgins; we tell our stories to whoever will listen; when we are older, we parade about with much younger lovers, just to prove to others that we really are what women expect us to be.

'But do you know something? That's simply not true. We understand nothing. We think that sex and *ejaculation are the same thing and, as you just said, they're not. We don't learn because we haven't the courage to say to the woman: show me your body. We don't learn because the woman doesn't have the courage to say: this is what I like. We are stuck with our primitive survival instincts, and that's that. Absurd though it may seem, do you know what is more important than sex for a man?'*

I thought it might be money or power, but I said nothing.

'Sport. Because a man can understand another man's body. We can see that sport is a dialogue between two bodies that understand each other.'

'You're mad.'

'Maybe. But it makes sense. Have you ever stopped to think about the feelings of the men you've been to bed with?'

'Yes, I have. They were all insecure. They were all afraid.'

'Worse than afraid, they were vulnerable. They didn't really know what they were doing, they only knew what society, friends and women themselves had told them was important. Sex, sex, sex, that's the basis of life, scream the advertisements, other people, films, books. No one knows what they're talking about. Since instinct is stronger than all of us, all they know is that it has to be done. And that's that.'

Enough. I had tried to give him lessons in sex in order to protect myself, now he was doing the same, and however wise our words – because each of us was always trying to impress the other – this was so stupid and so unworthy of our relationship! I drew him to me because – regardless of what he had to say or of what I thought about myself – life had taught me many things. In the beginning, everything was love and surrender. But then the serpent appeared and said to Eve: what you surrendered, you will lose. That is how it was with me – I was driven out of paradise when I was still at school, and ever since then, I have been trying to find a way of telling the serpent he was wrong, that living was more important than keeping things to yourself. But the serpent was right and I was wrong.

I knelt down and gradually took off his clothes, and I saw his penis there, sleeping and unresponsive. This didn't seem to bother him, and I kissed the inner part of his legs, starting at his feet. His penis slowly began to respond, and I touched it, then put it in my mouth and – unhurriedly, so that he wouldn't interpret this as: 'right, get ready for action!' – I kissed it with all the tenderness of someone who expects nothing in return, and for precisely that reason I got everything I wanted. I saw that he was getting excited, and he began to touch my nipples, circling them with his fingers as he had on that night of total darkness, making me want to have him again between my legs or in my mouth or whatever way he wanted to possess me.

He didn't take off my jacket; he had me lie face forwards, with the upper part of my body bent over the table, and my feet still on the floor. He penetrated me slowly and unhurriedly this time, no longer afraid of losing me, because, deep down, he too had realised that this was a dream and that it would always be a dream, and would never become reality.

At the same time as I felt him inside me, I was aware of his hand on my breasts, my buttocks, touching me as only a woman knows how. Then I knew that we were made for each other, because he could be a woman, as he was now, and I could be a man, as when we talked or when we initiated that joint search for the two lost souls, the two missing fragments needed to complete the universe.

As he simultaneously penetrated and touched me, I felt that he was doing this not only to me, but to the whole universe. We had time, tenderness and mutual knowledge. Yes, it had been good to arrive carrying two suitcases, ready to leave, and to be immediately thrown to the floor and penetrated with a kind of fearful urgency; but it was good too knowing that the night would never end and that there, on the kitchen table, orgasm wasn't a goal in itself, but the beginning of that encounter.

He stopped moving inside me while his fingers worked quickly and I had one, two, three orgasms in a row. I felt like pushing him away, for the pain of pleasure is so intense that it hurts, but I resisted; I accepted that this was how it was, that I could withstand another orgasm or another two, or even more ...

... and suddenly, a kind of light exploded inside me. I was no longer myself, but a being infinitely superior to everything I knew. When his hand took me to my fourth orgasm, I entered a place where everything seemed at peace, and with my fifth orgasm I knew God. Then I felt him beginning to move inside me again, although his hand had still not stopped, and I said 'Oh God', and surrendered to whatever came next, Heaven or Hell.

It was Heaven. I was the earth, the mountains, the tigers, the rivers that flowed into the lakes, the lakes that became the sea. He was thrusting faster and faster now, and the pain was mingled with pleasure, and I could have said: 'I can't take any more', but that would have been unfair, because, by then, he and I were one person.

I allowed him to penetrate me for as long as it took; his nails were now digging into my buttocks, and there I was face down on the kitchen table, thinking that there wasn't a better place in the world to make love. Again the creak of the table, his breathing growing ever faster, his nails bruising me, my sex beating hard against his, flesh against flesh, bone against bone, and I was about to have another orgasm, and so was he, and none of this, absolutely none of this was a LIE!

'Come on!'

He knew what he was saying, and I knew that this was the moment; I felt my whole body soften, I ceased to be myself – I was no longer listening, seeing or tasting anything – I was merely feeling.

'Come on!'

And I came at the same moment he came. It wasn't eleven minutes, it was an eternity, it was as if we had both left our bodies and were walking joyfully through the gardens of paradise in understanding and friendship. I was woman and man, he was man and woman. I don't know how long it lasted, but everything seemed to be silent, at prayer, as if the universe and life had ceased to exist and become transformed into something sacred, nameless and timeless.

But time returned, I heard his shouts and I shouted with him, the table legs beat on the floor, and it didn't occur to either of us to wonder what the rest of the world might be thinking.

And suddenly he withdrew from me and laughed; I felt my vagina contract, and I turned to him and I laughed too, and we embraced as if it were the first time we had made love in our entire lives.

'Bless me,' he said.

I blessed him, not really knowing what I was doing. I asked him to do the same, and he did, saying, 'blessed be this woman, who has loved much'. They were beautiful words, and we embraced again and stayed there, unable to understand how eleven minutes could carry a man and a woman so far.

Neither of us was tired. We went into the living room, he put on a record and did exactly as I had hoped: he lit the fire and poured me some wine. Then he opened a book and read:

A time to be born, and a time to die;
A time to plant, and a time to pluck up that which is
planted;
A time to kill, and a time to heal;
A time to break down, and a time to build up;
A time to weep, and a time to laugh;
A time to mourn, and a time to dance;
A time to cast away stones, and a time to gather
stones together;
A time to embrace, and a time to refrain from
embracing;
A time to get, and a time to lose;
A time to keep, and a time to cast away;
A time to rend, and a time to sew;
A time to keep silence, and a time to speak;
A time to love, and a time to hate;
A time of war, and a time of peace.

This sounded like a farewell, but it was the loveliest farewell I would ever experience in my life.

I embraced him and he embraced me, and we lay down on the carpet beside the fire. I was still filled by a sense of plenitude, as if I had always been a wise, happy, fulfilled woman.

'What made you fall in love with a prostitute?'

'I didn't understand it myself at the time. But I've thought about it since, and I think it was because, knowing that your body would never be mine alone, I had to concentrate on conquering your soul.'

'Weren't you jealous?'

'You can't say to the spring: "Come now and last as long as possible." You can only say: "Come and bless me with your hope, and stay as long as you can."'

Words lost on the wind. But I needed to hear them, and he needed to say them. I fell asleep, although I don't know when. I dreamed, not of a situation or of a person, but of a perfume that flooded the air.

When Maria opened her eyes, a few rays of sun were coming in through the open blinds.

'I've made love with him twice,' she thought, looking at the man asleep by her side. 'And yet it's as if we had always been together, and he had always known my life, my soul, my body, my light, my pain.'

She got up to go to the kitchen and make some coffee. That was when she saw the two suitcases in the hall and she remembered everything: her promise, the prayer she had said in the church, her life, the dream that insisted on becoming reality and losing its charm, the perfect man, the love in which body and soul were one and the same and in which pleasure and orgasm were different things.

She could stay; she had nothing more to lose, only an illusion. She remembered the poem: a time to weep, and a time to laugh.

But there was another line too: 'a time to embrace, and a time to refrain from embracing'. She made the coffee, shut the kitchen door and phoned for a taxi. She summoned all her willpower, which had carried her so far, and which was the source of energy for her 'light', which had told her the exact time to leave, which was protecting her and making her treasure forever the memory of that night. She got dressed, picked up her suitcases and left, hoping against hope that he would wake up and ask her to stay.

But he didn't wake up. While she was waiting for the taxi outside, a gypsy was passing, carrying bouquets of flowers.

'Would you like to buy one?'

Maria bought one; it was the sign that autumn had arrived and summer had been left behind. It would be a long time now before the café tables were out on the pavements in Geneva and the parks were full once more of people strolling about and sunbathing. It didn't matter; she was leaving because she had chosen to leave, and there was no reason for regrets.

She got to the airport, drank another cup of coffee and waited four hours for her flight to Paris, thinking all the time that he would arrive at any moment, because at some point before they fell asleep, she had told him the time of her flight. That's how it always happened in films: at the last moment, when the woman is just about to board the plane, the man races up to her, puts his arms around her and kisses her, and brings her back to his world, beneath the smiling, indulgent gaze of the flight staff. The words 'The End' appear on the screen, and the audience knows that, from then on, they will live happily ever after.

'Films never tell you what happens next,' she thought, trying to console herself. Marriage, cooking, children, ever more infrequent sex, the discovery of the first note from his mistress, the decision to confront him, his promise that it will never happen again, the second note from another mistress, another confrontation and this time a threat to leave him, this time the man reacts less vehemently and merely tells her that he loves her. The third note from a third mistress, and the decision to say nothing, to pretend that she knows nothing, because he might tell her that he doesn't love her any more and that she's free to leave.

No, films never show that. They finish before the real world begins. It's best not to think too much about it.

She read one, two, three magazines. In the end, they announced her flight, after almost an eternity in that airport lounge, and she got on the plane. She still imagined the famous scene in which, as she fastens her seatbelt, she feels a hand on her shoulder, turns round and there he is, smiling at her.

Nothing happened.

She slept on the short flight between Geneva and Paris. She hadn't had time to think about what she would tell them at home, what story she would invent, but her parents would probably just be happy to have their daughter back, and to have a farm and a comfortable old age ahead of them.

She woke up with the jolt of the plane landing. It taxied for a long time, and the flight attendant came to tell her that she would have to change terminals, because the flight to Brazil left from Terminal F and she was in Terminal C. But there was no need to worry; there were no delays, and she still had plenty of time, and if she wasn't sure where to go, the ground staff would help her.

While the passenger loading bridge was being put in place, she wondered if it would be worth spending a day in Paris, just to take some photographs and be able to tell people that she had been there. She needed time to think, to be alone with herself, to bury her memories of last night deep down inside her, so that she could use them whenever she needed to feel alive. Yes, a day in Paris was an excellent idea; she asked the flight attendant when the next flight to Brazil was, if she decided not to leave that day.

The flight attendant asked to see her ticket and said that, unfortunately, it didn't allow for that kind of stopover. Maria consoled herself with the thought that visiting such a beautiful city all on her own would only depress her. She was still managing to cling on to her sang-froid, to her willpower, and didn't want to ruin it all by seeing a beautiful view and missing someone intensely.

She got off the plane and went through the security checks; her luggage would go straight on to the next plane, so she didn't have to bother with that. The doors opened, the passengers emerged and embraced whoever was waiting for them, wife, mother, children. Maria pretended not to notice, at the same time pondering her own loneliness, except that this time she had a secret, a dream, which would make her solitude less bitter, and life would be easier.

'We'll always have Paris.'

The voice didn't belong to a tourist guide or to a taxi driver. Her legs shook when she heard it.

'We'll always have Paris?'

'It's a quote from one of my favourite films. Would you like to see the Eiffel Tower?'

Oh, yes, she would, she would love to. Ralf was holding a bunch of roses, and his eyes were full of light, the light she had seen on that first day, when he was painting her while the cold wind outside had made her feel awkward to be sitting there.

'How did you manage to get here before me?' she asked, merely to disguise her amazement; she wasn't in the least interested in the answer, but she needed a breathing space.

'I saw you reading a magazine at Geneva airport. I could have come over, but I'm such an incurable romantic that

I thought it would be best to catch the next shuttle to Paris, wander about the airport here for three hours, consult the arrivals screen over and over, buy some flowers, say the words that Rick says to his beloved in *Casablanca* and see the look of surprise on your face. And to be utterly sure that this was what you wanted, that you were expecting me, that all the determination and willpower in the world would not be enough to prevent love from changing the rules of the game from one moment to the next. It's really easy being as romantic as people in the movies, don't you think?'

She had no idea whether it was easy or difficult, and she didn't honestly care, even though she had only just met this man, even though they had made love for the first time only a few hours before, even though she had only been introduced to his friends the previous evening, even though he had been a regular at the nightclub where she had worked, even though he had been married twice. These were not exactly impeccable credentials. On the other hand, she now had enough money to buy a farm, she had her youth ahead of her, a great deal of experience of life and a great independence of soul. Nevertheless, as always happened when fate chose for her, she thought, once again, that she would take the risk.

She kissed him, utterly indifferent now to what happens after the words 'The End' appear on the cinema screen.

But if, one day, someone should decide to tell her story, she would ask them to begin it just as all the fairy tales begin:

Once upon a time ...

Afterword

Like everyone else – and in this case I have no qualms about generalising – it took me a long time to discover the sacred nature of sex. My youth coincided with an age of enormous freedom, great discoveries and many excesses, which was followed by a period of conservatism and repression – the price to be paid for extremes that brought with them some very harsh consequences indeed.

In that decade of excess (the 1970s), the writer Irving Wallace wrote a book about censorship in America, describing the legal shenanigans involved in preventing the publication of a book about sex: *The Seven Minutes*.

In Wallace's novel, the contents of the book which provokes the discussion about censorship are merely hinted at, and the subject of sexuality itself is rarely mentioned. I wondered what that banned book would be like; perhaps I could have a go at writing it myself.

However, in his novel, Wallace makes many references to this non-existent book, and this necessarily limited the task I had imagined, indeed, made it impossible. I was left with just the title (although I felt Wallace had made a rather conservative estimate of the time involved, and so decided to increase it) and the idea of how important it was to treat sexuality seriously – like many writers before me.

In 1997, after a lecture I gave in Mantua, Italy, I went back to my hotel and found that someone had left a manuscript for me in reception. Now, I never normally read unsolicited manuscripts, but I did read that one – the true story of a Brazilian prostitute, her marriages, her problems with the law, and her various adventures. In 2000, when I was passing through Zurich, I met that prostitute – known professionally as Sonia – and said how much I had liked what I had read. I suggested she send it to my Brazilian publisher, who, however, decided, in the end, not to publish it. Sonia was living in Italy at the time, but had travelled up on the train to meet me in Zurich. She invited us – myself, a friend and a female journalist from the newspaper *Blick*, who had just interviewed me – to go to Langstrasse, the local red light district. I didn't know that Sonia had already forewarned her colleagues of our visit, and to my surprise, I ended up signing several of my books, translated into various languages.

At that point, I had already decided to write about sex, but I still didn't have a plot or a principal character; I was thinking of something much more along the lines of the conventional search for sacredness, but that visit to Langstrasse taught me something: in order to write about the sacred nature of sex, it was necessary to understand why it had been so profaned.

In conversation with a journalist from the Swiss magazine, *L'Illustrée*, I described that spontaneous book-signing in Langstrasse, and he wrote a long article about it.

The result was that, at a book-signing in Geneva, several prostitutes turned up to have their copies of my books duly signed. I was very struck by one of them in particular, and afterwards – with my agent and friend, Mônica Antunes – we went for a coffee that turned into supper that turned into other meetings in the days that followed. Thus was born the connecting thread of *Eleven Minutes*.

I would like to thank Anna von Planta, my Swiss publisher, who supplied me with important facts about the legal situation of prostitutes in her country. I would also like to thank the following women in Zurich (using their *noms de guerre*): Sonia, whom I met for the first time in Mantua (who knows, maybe one day, someone will publish your book!), Martha, Antenora and Isabella. And in Geneva (again using their *noms de guerre*): Amy, Lucia, Andrei, Vanessa, Patrick, Thérèse and Anna Christina.

Many thanks also to Antonella Zara, who allowed me to use passages from her book, *The Science of Passion*, in certain sections of Maria's diary.

Finally, I must thank Maria (*nom de guerre*), who now lives in Lausanne with her husband and her two lovely daughters and who, during various meetings with myself and Mônica, told us her story, on which this book is based.

Paulo Coelho

The Alchemist

Paulo Coelho

Every few decades a book is published that changes the lives of its readers forever. Paulo Coelho's *The Alchemist* is such a book. With over 27 million copies sold worldwide, *The Alchemist* has already achieved the status of a modern classic.

This is the story of Santiago, an Andalusian shepherd boy who dreams of travelling the world in search of a treasure as extravagant as any ever found. From his home in Spain he journeys to the exotic markets of Tangiers and then into the Egyptian desert, where a fateful encounter with the alchemist awaits him.

The Alchemist is a transforming novel about the essential wisdom of listening to our hearts, learning to read the omens strewn along life's path and, above all, following our dreams.

By the River Piedra
I Sat Down and Wept

Paulo Coelho

By the River Piedra tells the story of Pilar, an independent and practical yet restless young woman, who is frustrated by the daily grind of university life and looking for greater meaning in her life. Pilar is transformed forever by an encounter with a childhood friend, now a mesmerising and handsome spiritual teacher – and a rumoured miracle worker – who leads her on a journey through the French Pyrenees, a magical landscape that has been home to holy visions and miracles through the ages.

The Fifth Mountain

Paulo Coelho

Fleeing his home from persecution, 23-year-old Elijah takes refuge with a young widow and her son in the beautiful town of Akbar. Already struggling to maintain his sanity in a chaotic world of tyranny and war, he is now forced to choose between his new-found love and his overwhelming sense of duty.

Evoking all the drama and intrigue of the colourful, chaotic world of the Middle East, Paulo Coelho turns the trials of Elijah into an intensely moving and inspiring story – one that powerfully brings out the universal themes of how faith and love can ultimately triumph over suffering.

The Pilgrimage

Paulo Coelho

On a legendary road across Spain, travelled by pilgrims of San Tiago, we find Paulo Coelho on a contemporary quest for ancient wisdom. This journey becomes a truly initiatory experience, and Paulo is transformed forever as he learns to understand the nature of truth through the simplicity of life.

The Pilgrimage has a very important place in the work of Paulo Coelho, not just because it is the first of his major books, but because of the way in which it expresses the humanity of Paulo's philosophy and the depth of his search.

The Valkyries

Paulo Coelho

This true record of an exotic odyssey is a profound work that
will enchant and thrill the reader.

Haunted by a devastating curse, Paulo is instructed by his
mysterious spiritual teacher to embark upon a journey to find
and speak to his guardian angel in an attempt to confront
and overcome his dark past. *The Valkyries* is a compelling
account of this journey, which takes him, with his wife Chris,
on a forty-day quest into the searing heat of the Mojave
Desert.

At once a modern-day adventure, a metaphysical battle
with self-doubt and fear and a true story of two people striv-
ing to understand one another, *The Valkyries* is ultimately a
story about forgiving our past and believing our future.

Veronika Decides to Die

Paulo Coelho

Veronika seems to have everything she could wish for. She is young and pretty, has plenty of attractive boyfriends, goes dancing, has a steady job, a loving family. Yet Veronika is not happy; something is lacking in her life. On the morning of November 11th, 1997, she decides to die. She takes an overdose of sleeping pills, only to wake up some time later in Villete, the local hospital. There she is told that although she is alive now her heart is damaged and she has only a few days to live ...

This story follows Veronika through these intense days as, to her surprise, she finds herself drawn into the enclosed world of Villete. She begins to notice more, to become interested in the other patients. She starts to see her past relationships much more clearly and understand why she had felt her life had no meaning. In this heightened state, Veronika discovers things she has never really allowed herself to feel before: hatred, fear, curiosity, love – even sexual awakening. Against all odds, she finds she is falling in love and wanting, if at all possible, to live again ...

The Devil and Miss Prym

Paulo Coelho

A stranger arrives in the small mountain village of Viscos. He carries with him a backpack containing a notebook and eleven gold bars. He comes searching for the answer to a question that torments him: are human beings, in essence, good or evil? In welcoming the mysterious foreigner, the whole village become accomplices to his sophisticated plot, which will forever mark their lives.

In this stunning new novel, Paulo Coelho's unusual protagonist sets the town a moral challenge from which they may never recover. A fascinating meditation on the human soul, *The Devil and Miss Prym* illuminates the reality of good and evil within us all, and our uniquely human capacity to choose between them.

Manual of the Warrior of Light

Paulo Coelho

Manual of the Warrior of Light is an invitation to each of us to live our dream, to embrace the uncertainty of life and to rise to meet our own unique destiny. In his inimitable style, Paulo Coelho helps us to discover the warrior of light within each of us.

With inspiring short passages, we are invited to embark upon the way of the warrior: the one who appreciates the miracle of being alive, the one who accepts failure, and the one whose quest leads him to become the person he wants to be.